A NEWLY-WEBS MIDLIFE

WITCHING AFTER FORTY
BOOK FOURTEEN

LIA DAVIS

L.A. BORUFF

CHAPTER ONE

"I almost don't want to leave." I slid my arm around Drew's waist as we walked the footpath back to the castle that had been converted into an inn. There were several cottages near the main castle, all dating back to the mid-seventeenth century.

The castle cat, who I'd been calling Nix, peered out of a window high in the turret. I could just see her little black face peering down. She'd been a constant companion over the last few weeks. Drew and I had spent the most wonderful time here, relaxing, eating far too much, and taking advantage of the castle's many amenities. I'd never had so many massages in my life.

The Andarsan was gorgeous inside and out. It

was nestled in the Highlands and sat on a loch. We'd spent a significant amount of time doing indoor activities to work off the delicious food. We'd also spent time on the loch in kayaks or paddle boarding.

This was a picture-perfect location for a honeymoon...if it hadn't been for the ghosts. That part had been a surprise.

The castle was *very* haunted. It tracked that a castle *that* old, even a small one like this, would have seen its fair share of death.

If I were human, I wouldn't have noticed the wandering spirits. I would've spent three weeks basking in my new husband's love and soaking up every possible amenity.

But I wasn't human, was I? I was half witch, half necromancer. Heavy on the necro power. In fact, my ex-roomie and mentor, Owen, had told me on several occasions that I was the most powerful necromancer he'd ever heard of. According to him, my father's side of the family—where my dead death powers came from—was one of the oldest bloodlines.

Everything I'd learned about my family since Owen had first told me that tracked. I'd found out that our necromancer lineage dated as far back as the freaking Vikings.

In fact, I'd recently learned that Alfred and I

were related. I was still digesting that one. Alfred, the ghoul I'd inherited from another necromancer. We'd since given Alfred his old body back, in a manner of speaking. He looked like his old self, anyway. And his old self was gorgeous.

My mother and Aunt had done a ritual that had basically put them in new bodies, and ever since, Alfred and my Aunt Winnie were, to be frank, disgustingly in love. Like teenagers who couldn't keep their hands off of each other. It was nice to not have to see that for three weeks, but time was starting to run short. We would have to go back to reality sooner or later.

"I won't miss all the ghosts, but yeah, it'll be hard to go back to work." Drew gave me a little squeeze as we made our way to the onsite restaurant, and the source of all the good food we'd eaten. Except for a few excursions into the village, we'd mostly let the castle chef make our culinary dreams come true.

It would be hard getting back to our lives when we returned home, but we had to eventually. This honeymoon had been like someone had pressed pause on all the chaos in our world. No doubt when we returned home the pandemonium would slap us in the face.

The slow pace since we arrived had been nice.

Although I did miss my family and friends at home. Mmm, not enough to leave yet, however. We had a couple more nights.

My phone chimed as we entered the restaurant through its enormous oak doors. They were at least ten feet tall and opened into a great hall of a dining room, decorated in a lot of wood and gilding. It put me in mind of how it must've looked in its heyday when lords and ladies dined before hosting great balls.

Along the front windows were intimate tables for couples to sit and enjoy the view of the loch. There was a great table for the communal dinners they frequently had, and all around that were tables for smaller parties who might not want to join in the middle. It was a great setup. Drew and I had taken our meals at the various locations, sometimes socializing, sometimes sitting together intimately.

I glanced at the message and smiled while Drew talked with the hostess. It was from Wallie and Michelle and had an audio message attached.

Once we were seated at our table, one of the cozy ones by the window, I played the audio. Of course, it started out loud, drawing the attention of others around us. I ducked my head, whispered, "Sorry," and turned down the volume so only Drew and I could hear.

The rapid sound of a heartbeat flowed out of my phone as I grinned like an idiot at Drew. "That's the sound of our grandbaby." I almost squealed but caught myself before I yelled out. I did let a tiny whisper of a sound come out. I couldn't help myself. My heart was beating almost as fast as the sound coming through the phone's speaker. My grand-daughter. Oh, my.

Drew's smile grew into amazement as he listened, then replayed it again and again. "It's so fast."

"That's normal," I said after he handed my phone back to me. I reopened my messaging app to text the kids back. "Especially since the baby is a girl. Their heartbeats tend to be faster." Wallie and Michelle weren't kids technically, but they would always be my babies. And yes, I was claiming Michelle as one of mine. She was having my first grandbaby, after all.

Wow. Such a strong heartbeat. It sounds magical. Name?

Wallie texted back quickly. **Yes, she definitely is magical. No name yet, but we have time to figure that out.**

My grin was probably sappy and huge, but I didn't care a bit. **She'll be here before you know it. We're at dinner, so I'll talk to you two later. Hugs!**

I set my phone on the table between Drew and me as a tingle crawled up my spine. I glanced around the dining room trying to pinpoint the source of my ghostly spidey senses. There were no ghosts in the restaurant, or at least there shouldn't have been any. I'd warded the place after the first time we'd eaten here. The last thing I needed was ghosts staring at me while I enjoyed my dinner. It made for difficult digestion.

The ward only worked while I was actually in the dining room. The rest of the time, the haints could do their worst with the other, oblivious diners. They couldn't really hurt them.

Unfortunately, even when I *was* here in the dining area, some ghosts figured out how they could ignore the magical warning to stay out. Inevitably, one or two made their way in. Maybe they were the stronger ones? I didn't know enough about ghosts to be sure. Probably something I should study, eventually.

My gaze landed on a man sitting alone. There was a half-eaten meal in front of him, and he seemed sad. More than that. He was grieving. The emotions flowed off him, reaching out to my overly sensitive empathy. Maybe his intense sadness was making my ghost radar go off.

I'd been in his shoes before, so full of grief and regret I couldn't see past it. When my Clay died, I'd thought I was drowning.

Drew covered my fingers, drawing my attention to him. He lifted my hand and kissed my knuckles. Warmth flowed through me as I leaned in to press my lips to his.

My husband.

I was still getting used to being married to Sheriff Drew Walker.

Our relationship had been a bit of a whirlwind. It had only been a little over a year since we'd met. What an incredible year it had been. I'd reconnected with my necromancer powers, become close to my now best friend Olivia, adopted Zoey and Larry and Alfred and Michelle and Lucy-Fur and Lucifer and my Uncle Wade. Plus my Mom, Aunt Winnie, and Dad were essentially back from the dead.

It'd been an absolutely insane year. And through it all, Drew had been there. My constant. My rock. The handsomest, kindest, everythingest man I'd known since my dear late husband Clay died six years ago. I couldn't help but stare into his vivid blue eyes and thank my lucky stars I'd come home to Shipton Harbor when I did... before some other woman snapped him up.

After we finished eating, we made our way to our room, which had a waterfront view. It was also, *most* unfortunately the ghost's favorite place to hang out, which made sexy time for hubby and me a little bit interesting. These ghosts didn't seem to care much about my wards. Sure, I could've forced them to leave. But they usually came back ten minutes later, and sometimes when they came back, they were aggravated and loud.

Once inside our room, Drew backed me up to the door and kissed me. I threaded my fingers in his hair and pulled him closer. When he ended the kiss, I smirked at him. "Hurry get under the blankets before the ghosts show up."

He wiggled his eyebrows, then pulled me behind him to do exactly as I'd said.

I JERKED awake but wasn't sure why at first. The first few days we'd woken up here, I'd been super disoriented, but it hadn't taken long to acclimate.

Tonight was a different story. I was befuddled until I saw a dead woman standing over me. We stared at each other for a long few moments. What in the world did this one want? Most of the specters here had just been bent on disruption and irritation. Or they only wanted to live out their afterlives alone, in relative peace.

This ghost was different. It was like she was actually looking at me. She had her black hair put up in a neat bun and wore an elaborate floor-length ballgown. I didn't know much about ballgowns, but it sure looked like expensive material to me. It had a tight bodice and a long, flowing skirt. In one hand she carried a mask that looked like it came from a masquerade ball.

As impressive as she looked, I was far too sleepy to fool with the crazy lady. "Go away. I'm sleeping." I tried to roll over, planning on ignoring the ghost, but she placed a hand on my arm. Uuuugh. It was cold and so icky when they touched me.

I sat up with a sigh, causing Drew to wake. He rolled over and then flopped back on the bed. "Not now. Why can't they ever come to visit while we're awake?"

"They do. But most of them don't actually try to interact."

The woman just stared at me, so I gave her a magical boost so we could talk. She obviously wanted something, and I didn't feel like trying to sleep with her standing over me or maybe touching me again. "What do you want?"

One rule about dealing with ghosts was don't be nice to them or you'd get a tagalong. For life and beyond. They liked to linger.

"Follow me," the woman said, then floated through the door to our room.

"This one's used to people doing what she says," Drew muttered. "Figures."

After a quick glance at each other, we pulled on our robes and headed out of the room. Drew leaned in and whispered, "This isn't a lady in white thing, is it?"

"The urban legend?" I asked. He nodded and I replied, "Gods, I hope not."

The ghost woman reappeared at the end of the hallway, waiting for us. Drew and I rushed to her as quietly as possible since it was the middle of the night. The castle was old and a bit creaky. The hardwood floors had been beautifully restored, but some things couldn't be restored in a building this ancient.

We tracked her to what seemed to be the unused portion of the castle. We'd explored here before, but it had felt like it was a section that the guests weren't meant to be in. Some of the rooms we passed looked like they were used for storage while others looked to be under construction or being remodeled.

We turned a corner and followed the ghost down yet another long hallway. Geez, how big was this place?

At the end of this one, the ghost stopped at a set of stairs, looking down them with a mix of anger and sadness. "Here," she said in an ethereal voice. The moment Drew and I reached the stairs, the ghost disappeared. It didn't take long to see why.

At the bottom of the stairs was the man from dinner, the one who had been so sad. He was crying over a woman's body. From the awkward position of the body, I had to guess she had fallen down the stairs.

Moonlight shone through a nearby window, illuminating the poor dead woman. She wore a white nightgown and had blond hair really close to the color of Olivia's hair. From this angle, it was almost a little unnerving. It could've been my bestie, except I knew she was home safe in Maine with her newly-turned-vampire husband Sam and her mother and father, *the* devil and his fae lady.

Moving my gaze from the woman, I studied the

man. "That's the guy from dinner," I whispered to Drew.

Drew made a soft grunt noise. "Yeah, but I didn't see her with him."

"Neither did I." I descended the stairs with Drew close behind, walking on my tiptoes to be as quiet as possible. When we reached the bottom, the man didn't even glance over at us. He just stared at the woman's body with tears rolling down his cheeks. I wondered if she was his wife or girlfriend. Daughter, maybe? It was kind of hard to tell ages when she was dead.

I moved closer until I was almost touching them. Still, he didn't look up. Nothing I did seemed to bring him out of his shock. Or was it grief that had frozen him into place?

"Sir," I prompted without a reaction. "Excuse me, sir?" He still didn't look over. This dude was seriously upset.

"Careful," Drew said. "Maybe he was sad at dinner because he knew he was going to have to kill her tonight."

A chilling thought. I bent down and touched the woman, pushing my magic into her. Maybe the deceased could tell me what happened to her.

She opened her eyes and sat straight, locking

gazes with me. "You didn't save her. You couldn't save her."

What the freaking frack? Before I could ask her what she meant, she fell back against the floor, dead once more. I tried to animate her again and had the same result with the same cryptic message. She wouldn't respond otherwise.

Who were we supposed to have saved? Not her, surely, or she would've said *me*.

Drew tapped me on the shoulder. "Don't touch anything else. We have to report this."

Nodding, I stood and used my magic to erase all evidence that I'd touched the body. While Drew called the police, I moved to the man. He'd moved away from the woman but still sat nearby, staring at her.

"Hello. Did you know her?" It seemed like a silly question, but I really wasn't sure if he'd known her or was just sad that she died. He could've been the first to find her and it shocked him into this stupor.

He didn't answer so Drew tried. "What's your name?"

Nothing. Drew and I shared a look. Drew motioned with his head for me to follow, and we moved to stand a few feet away. "This whole thing is weird," I said.

"And that is seriously saying something considering what we deal with on a daily basis."

"True," Drew agreed with a chuckle. "I feel like something isn't quite right with this."

"Yeah, and I'm not talking about the dead body."

When I looked back to try to talk to the man again, I gasped. He was gone.

Oh, yeah. That wasn't suspicious at all.

CHAPTER TWO

I t was late morning before I crawled my sleepy self out of bed and stumbled to the shower. But sleeping late wasn't unusual for me, especially since we'd been on our honeymoon. I just wished I'd gotten more sleep actually *during* the night. I was frikkin' exhausted, even after sleeping late.

But at least I felt more human. Well, as human as I ever was, now that I had some coffee in me. Drew had gotten up before me, no surprise there. He was such an overachiever. I loved him in spite of it. He'd gotten me a gigantic cup of coffee. I sucked down another long drink and sighed. The man was definitely a keeper. He needed a gift. Maybe I could swing a solo trip into town before it was time to go home. He had said something about a few rounds of golf. If I got him busy with that I'd go see about a just-because-I-love-you present.

I had just pulled my jeans over my hips when the ghost woman from last night appeared in front of me again. "Fu—" I cut myself off with a growl. Just like in the middle of last night, she still wore her floor-length gown. It had jewels all over it. Now in the daylight, I could actually see a floral design down one side, too. It was stunning. The formal gown's design didn't help me try to pinpoint when she'd died. If she'd been in normal clothes, it might've been easy. But expensive ball gowns didn't seem to change too much over the years. Not to my inexperienced eyes, anyway. Fashionista I was not.

She stared at me while I zipped up and buttoned my jeans. I raised a brow at her. "Morning."

"You must save them," she said. "You're the only one who can help."

It had probably been difficult for her to say that much. I reached out to give her some power in hopes that it would clear her mind enough to explain what she wanted, but she disappeared before I could ask any questions.

Well, then. Okie dokie. How the heck were we supposed to help when we didn't know what the problem was? And why me? Why was I the only one?

Cause it was always me, that's why. Ugh.

Probably she was coming to me because I was the first necromancer to stay at the resort. That made the most sense. Lucky me.

Drew stepped out of the bathroom, and I drank him in, momentarily forgetting how to breathe, much less what the bejeweled party lady wanted. He'd emerged with a white towel wrapped around his waist and his short brown hair was wet and going all over the place.

Have I mentioned that he was ripped? The man worked out daily. Dollars to donuts, that man had been in the resort gym this morning while I snoozed the day away and dreamed about a French toast breakfast.

The term silver fox had been created for men like him. I needed to send his photo to Webster's to go beside the term in the dictionary.

Drew smirked at me as he slowly removed his towel, rubbing it along his chest with the towel hanging down to obscure the part I wanted to see. He twisted around, still hiding all the pieces I wanted, to hang it on the bathroom door. *Finally*, he turned, giving me the money shot. Oh, yeah.

"Ava?" He snapped his fingers. "My eyes are up here. Who were you talking to?"

"Ghost lady." I sipped my coffee and watched him dress with disappointment. He wasn't in the mood, apparently. I could've changed his mind, but I still needed a good shower, too. Maybe later. "She said something to the effect of only me being able to save them." We spent a couple minutes going over who them could've been. "I think I'll call home and check on things. Maybe Mom has some ideas on how to get the ghost to talk." She'd lived for years on the ghostly plane, which we called the Inbetween. She knew stuff.

"Good idea. I'll go and call the authorities to see if they have any other information about the dead woman." He leaned in and kissed me on the lips, letting it linger a bit.

"Do you think the ghost lady and the couple from last night are connected? Other than the ghost led us to the crime scene."

"Surely they are." He shrugged. "Why else would a ghost tell you, of all people, about a dead woman?"

"Yeah, I guess that was a stupid question."

Drew stopped short, turned to me, and put one finger under my chin to lift my gaze. "It was not. We shouldn't discount the fact that it could in theory be unrelated. With us, we can never tell." He dropped a soft kiss onto my forehead. I watched him grab his phone and head out into the hallway. Then I called home to tell everyone about the craziness of the ghost. Alfred, my beloved Viking ghoul, answered.

"Alfred, I think this honeymoon is cursed," I said as a greeting. "We're being haunted by a ghost."

"That does sound like quite a problem," Alfred said. "I'm sure you can handle it." His squeaky voice had all the confidence in the world.

I appreciated his certainty of my abilities, even if I didn't always feel the same way. "Is my mom around?"

"She's in the kitchen. I'll get her for you." He set the phone down, and I listened for background noise. Everything seemed to be quiet.

A few moments later, my mom was on the phone. "Hi, honey," she said. "What's going on?"

I quickly related the story of the ghost woman and what she'd said. My mom had been a ghost before I'd animated her and magically placed her spirit into another body. So, she'd know more about ghost behavior than me.

"It sounds like she wants you to help her solve a problem," my mom said. "I'm not sure what you can do to get her to talk more. Especially if she is avoiding your magic as you explained. You might have to solve this mystery the old-fashioned way."

I'd been afraid of that. It was the only explanation for why she kept moving away or disappearing when I tried to use magic.

At least I had a sheriff to help me with the detective work. Maybe someone here knew the woman who died last night. If we knew more about her, then we might be able to figure out how the ghost lady was connected. "Great. Thanks," I said in a flat, teasing tone. "How is everything there?"

"It's good. Don't worry about us. Enjoy your new husband and your alone time with him."

I was for sure doing that. Now we had a mystery to solve. We'd at least do it together. "Okay, if you say so. I'll talk to you later. Love you, Mom."

"Love you, too, sweetie."

I hung up and turned around. Shrieking, I dropped my phone as my heart jumped out of my chest. Luci was lounging on the bed, eating popcorn like he'd been here the whole time and belonged nowhere else. He wore black skinny jeans and a white t-shirt with a black leather jacket thrown over it. His hair was bleached blond and styled in its signature coif. "What's shakin'?" he asked around a mouthful of popcorn.

I eyed him and asked, "What are you wearing? You look like you just left the set of Grease if Grease was starring David Bowie."

He winked at me. "I was at a punk concert last night. It was killer." He threw up the devil's horns with his fingers. "It was like they were saluting me all night!"

I rolled my eyes and said, "Of course, you had to dress the part. You're lucky I don't have time to deal with you right now."

He jumped up and looked around, spotting the very large, full-length mirror on the wall. It was old as crap, and I was pretty sure the frame was at least gold leaf if not somehow real gold. If that was even possible. Whatever it was, it looked expensive. "This will do," he mumbled and waved his hand over the front of it. A shimmering portal appeared in it. The glass had been slightly warped with little black dots on it. I could still see them faintly behind the portal. At least he hadn't damaged the antique.

Probably hadn't. *Probably* hadn't damaged it.

Peering over his shoulder, I furrowed my brow when I recognized the room. "Is that a view from the big mirror in my bathroom?" I asked. "What did you do?" And why did he do it?

He ignored me as he shivered and scanned the hotel room. "Yeesh. This place is way too haunted for me. Laters, baby." And with that, he stepped through the portal he'd created in the big mirror on the wall of the ancient castle and disappeared.

Typical Luci.

I stared at the mirror portal like I expected a creature to come out of it. Heck, it connected to my house. There was every possibility a creature of varying deadness could come out.

Rolling my eyes, I went to the desk by the large picture window and sat down to check my email while I waited for Drew to come back.

"Did someone say ghosts?" I didn't have to turn around to know it was my bestie.

I burst out laughing and whirled around in the desk chair. Of *course*, Olivia would be interested in this. Heck, I was glad she was here. I'd missed her cheery personality and how she loved to spout random facts. "Welcome to the honeymoon. A ghost visited us last night and again this morning."

"What did it want?" she asked, her blue eyes wide with excitement.

"I don't know," I said, chuckling as she caught

sight of the room. As she oohed and ahhed over the four-poster bed and giant tapestry, I gave her the play-by-play of the events in the last twelve hours.

When I finished, she jumped off the bed. She'd been testing the mattress. "Wow. I'm so glad I came to help solve a mystery," she exclaimed. "Let's go interview the staff."

CHAPTER THREE

"Where is Sammie?" I asked Olivia, amusement lighting up my insides at Olivia's excitement. She had that effect on me. I'd felt burdened before. Now I wanted to go gung-ho with her to figure it out. Olivia was good for me.

"He's with Phira in Faery for a few days for some camping thing they're doing." She smiled and added, "Besides, I had some free time and needed a break from clingy Sam, love his heart."

Poor Sam. My best friend since we were in diapers had been turned into a vampire when we'd gone to Milan to free the necromancers the vampire council had imprisoned.

Our friend Jax, who was the vampire leader of

the United States, turned him after he'd almost died during the fight with the bad vampires.

Since being turned, Sam had been stuck up Olivia's behind. She had been used to him working long hours as a police officer, but now he was home all the time since he couldn't work during the day. Baby vamps sleep during the hours of sunlight. They had no control over that. As soon as the sun came up, they conked out like flipping off their light switch.

We'd found out when Jax and Hailey came to our wedding that Olivia was Sam's fated mate, which was a vampire and shifter thing. His need to bond with her, despite already being married to her, was strong. He'd never felt it before being turned, and if he hadn't been made into a bloodsucker, he never would've felt it. He was overprotective—far more so than usual—and didn't like to be separated from her for very long.

Olivia was still adjusting to all the attention, which she normally loved, but she'd also been trying to focus on being a good mom. That was something she felt like she'd failed with her first two kids, Jess and Devan.

I had faith in my two besties that they will find their balance again. "How did you escape Sam?"

Olivia grinned and peered into the small bathroom. "Wade distracted him with finding the perfect location for the new vamp bar."

"Good for them. I'm so happy they're going to be working together like this."

My deceased husband's uncle, Wade, whom I claimed as my own uncle long ago, had been turned into a vampire back in March when I'd gone to Philly to sell my house. He'd been turned by a rouge vamp. I'd helped Jax catch the rogue, which had actually been a lot of fun. I'd figured out then that necromancers could control vampires, since blood-suckers were dead. Or more technically, undead.

"I'm glad you could come and help us out," I said. "This place is a little bit haunted."

"No kidding," Olivia said as she looked around the room, pulling the tapestry back from the wall. "Darn. No hidden passage. So, what do we know so far?"

"Well, not much, actually," I admitted. "I guess we need to find out who the dead woman is. Drew went on a walk to call the local cops to see what he can find out."

"And how she died," Olivia said. "Although, I have a feeling the fall down the stairs might've had some contribution to it."

I nodded and snorted. "Yeah, me too. Let's go talk

to the manager and see if we can get some more information."

When I finally pulled Olivia away from knocking on the walls, we went downstairs and found the manager.

He was a middle-aged man with graying hair. "Hello, Niko, how are you?"

He smiled warmly at me. "Mrs. Walker. What can I do for you this morning?" He'd been the kindest since we'd arrived.

"This is my good friend Olivia Thompson."

Niko's face lit up. "Mrs. Thompson. Will you be staying with us?"

She shook her head as she took Niko's hand. "No, I'm just here for a visit."

I leaned forward conspiratorially. "We came down to ask you about the woman who died last night."

His face fell. "Terrible business, that. Simply terrible. She was staying here." He dry-washed his hands and bit his lip. "Am I a terrible person for being worried about what it's going to do to our bookings if this gets out?"

"No," Olivia and I said at the same time.

We chuckled and Olivia said, "Not at all. You can have empathy for the woman's family and friends while also being concerned about your own livelihood."

He gave her a grateful smile. "Her name was Annette. She'd been staying here at the resort on a writing retreat."

Oh, a writing retreat. That sounded like exactly what I needed to do to get my next book off the ground. I'd had a hard time getting into it.

"Did you know her?" I asked. "Were you familiar with her work?"

The manager shook his head. "I'm afraid not," he said. "She kept to herself mostly. I only spoke to her a few times, though she was kind during those conversations."

"Do you know if she was having any problems with anyone?" Olivia asked. "Any conflicts or anything?"

Again, the manager shook his head. "I'm sorry, but I don't know," he said. "Like I said, she kept to herself."

"What about the man we saw with her?" I asked, then described the man. "Did you see him? Do you know who he is?"

The manager's eyebrows furrowed in confusion. "What man?" he asked. "I didn't see anyone matching that description." He tapped on the computer keyboard behind the counter, then shook his head again. "We have a lot of guests right now, but I don't think any of them match that description."

Olivia and I exchanged a glance. This was getting strange. Why would the manager say he hadn't seen the man when we saw him ourselves? Unless...

"We should go," Olivia said suddenly. She must've had the same thought I had. "I think we're done here."

I nodded and we thanked the manager before walking toward the front doors. Once we were outside, Olivia turned to me. "That was weird," she said. "Why would he lie about seeing the man?"

"I don't know," I said. "But I have a feeling we're not going to get any more information from him." It seemed too unlikely that Niko had never seen one of his own customers.

"So, what now?" Olivia asked.

"I guess we need to find out more about Annette," I said. "See if we can figure out why she was really here."

Olivia's eyes sparked with her fae magic, and she gave me a slow, mischievous smile. "We should break into her room and nose around."

I laughed. "I was just going to suggest that." Great minds.

She threaded an arm around mine and led me back inside and down the hall to the elevators. "If we're gonna share a brain, we might want to try to get one that works."

CHAPTER FOUR

Olivia used her magic to get Annette's room number, a nifty little trick her biological father, Lucifer, had shown her. It involved astral projection and a bit of possession, so I wasn't sure it was something I wanted to learn, even if I could. Probably, I wasn't even capable anyway.

On our way to the floor Annette's room was on, I texted Drew to meet us there. Hopefully, after this long, he'd be done talking to the police, but I knew my Drew. He could go on and on about a case for hours. He and Sam sometimes got on a roll. When that happened, Olivia and I generally snuck out to do our own thing.

My hunky hubby was waiting on us when we arrived. Grabbing his hand, I beamed up at him.

"How did you get here so fast?" I wanted to touch him all the time. I'd wanted to do that before we were married, too, but here in the romantic castle, it was stronger.

He held out a key, looking a little too triumphant. "I'm helping with the investigation. I spent most of the morning having my credentials sent over so I could be given privileges with the local DCI. That's what they call their detective force." His grin widened." Hunters aren't without our own tricks."

Boy, did I know that. After having the Walker family stay with us for the wedding, I could write a book on hunters and their tricks. When they'd taken on the tentacle monster that had escaped from Hell during the rehearsal dinner, the hunters had seemed to conjure weapons left and right. Their skills were limitless. As was their ability to be grumpy, but that was another story.

I waved a hand toward the door and said, "Shall we go in?"

He handed Olivia and me gloves to put on, then opened the room. "We might as well do this right." Inside was clean even though the maid hadn't been in, since it was a crime scene.

"Forensics has already been in, but still don't

move anything," Drew said as he put his own gloves on.

He started with a quick scan of the room, using his hunter's instincts while Olivia and I looked around with our own flares of magic and investigative eyes.

Olivia headed over to the closet while I sat down at the desk and opened the laptop that had been left sitting there. It fired to life instantly, indicating she hadn't turned it off when she'd last used it. It was only in sleep mode. In this day and age, computers were a great source of info about a person. At the least, I'd be able to find out if she was emailing anyone. Or maybe if she'd had any inkling that something bad was going to happen. Sometimes people had premonitions. Heck, I knew how to raise skeletons from the dead. A little premonition wasn't anything shocking.

The victim's screen saver was a picture of a castle in Scotland. In fact, it was The Andarsan—the very one we were staying at. That made me wonder if this had been the first time she'd stayed here. However, she was an author. It was more likely that she'd been using this castle as the inspiration for her next book.

After the second try at the password, I sat back in

the chair, afraid to attempt it again. If I did it too many times, the computer might shut down completely. "Either of you know how to magically hack into a computer?"

Drew came to look over my shoulder. Then he moved the computer so he could type. "Let me try something." He winked and typed in some kind of code.

I laughed. He really never ceased to amaze. "Is computer hacking a required skill for hunters?"

Drew grinned and kissed my cheek. "I can teach you to do it. It's a handy skill to have."

Yeah, if you wanted to go to prison for it. Then again, I was married to a sheriff. Drew was pretty tech-savvy, but the computer hacker side gig was new news for me. "What else do I not know about you?" I tried not to sound accusing. We'd only been together for a year. We were bound to continue to learn things about one another for a while, at least.

He frowned and averted his gaze. A spike of guilt rushed through our magical bond, so I touched his hand, forcing him to look at me. "I know you held back your hunter abilities from me, and I'm okay with that because I trust you to fill me in before I actually *need* to know." I trusted him completely. That was the important part. He didn't like talking about his hunter life. In his defense, he'd walked away from the hunter life years ago. It really didn't matter to me what he could do. Besides, I could feel his intentions through our bond.

"You may get a crash course sooner than later," he said flatly.

I knew what he meant. Now that his family had accepted me and all my weirdness, Drew had warned me that they would probably try to pass on missions that were near us. After all, they had recruited Owen to work with them full-time. That was probably really good for my best necromancer friend, though. He needed more purpose in life. To feel helpful and useful.

Drew wouldn't go hunting without me. We'd already agreed that if he did return to doing any hunting, it would be with us as a team.

Instead of returning the laptop to me, he searched through her folders until he found something he deemed interesting—a partial manuscript.

"What's this?" I asked as I started reading it. "Annette was writing a murder mystery."

The victim in the story was described as a beautiful socialite who'd been killed in her room at a castle in the Scottish highlands.

Olivia had come out of the closet by then and she

said, "I found something, too. Research notes about a blonde woman falling down the stairs every ten years since the sixties." Olivia handed me a folder. I rifled through it and found newspaper clippings and photos, some of them original, some photocopied. Skimming the dates, I nodded. "Yeah, the first article is in the sixties. This is nuts."

Drew and I exchanged a look. This just kept getting weirder and weirder. What would we find next, that the castle cat was a ghost?

CHAPTER FIVE

The three of us huddled together in Annette's room to read through the newspaper clippings. One, in particular, caught my attention, about a woman who'd fallen down a set of stairs and broken her neck two days before Halloween in 1961. I picked up a picture of a woman who could have passed for Olivia's doppelganger. It also looked somewhat like the woman who we'd found dead last night.

"Wow," I said, handing her the photo. "She sort of looks like you, Olivia."

"Not all blondes look alike," she said with a roll of her eyes and flipped her hair over her shoulder. She eyed the photo like it was some dark omen or something. "I'm far more attractive."

Once we'd at least glanced at each article, Drew took the photo and the articles and stuffed them back into the folder. Then he pulled out a flash drive from his pants pocket.

"You just carry a flash drive around with you?" I teased, wondering what else he was going to pull out of his pants.

Well, there was one thing I'd like for him to pop out, but not in front of Olivia. Maybe we could find a dark corner of the castle to act inappropriately in later.

Drew flashed me a grin. He knew what I was thinking about. "Get your mind out of the gutter. It's one of my keychains. I took to carrying it around years ago. It helps me sometimes at work." He stuck the drive into the USB port and copied her hard drive.

And here I'd been thinking he'd conjured it. He rarely openly used his magic, and I'd been wondering if he'd start now because his family had accepted me. I hoped he would. Hunters had more magic than Drew used. I was sure about that.

Instead of opening that can of worms, I said, "Let's go downstairs and see if the staff can tell us more about the woman killed sixty years ago. I bet there's at least one or two who have heard the story."

We turned to leave the room just as the sound of a high-pitched scream echoed throughout the room.

Olivia jumped and clung to my arm as the dark-haired woman who'd woken me up in the middle of the night appeared. "Get out!" she screamed and then disappeared.

"Well that was rude," Olivia said, releasing my arm.

I nodded. "She was the ghost who woke us last night. This morning she told me to help them. Whoever them are. I still have no idea."

The last thing I needed was to deal with a bipolar ghost with mood swings. I wasn't a ghost expert but felt obligated to help solve this case.

"She's not scaring us off the case now." Drew opened the door and held it for Olivia and me. "If anything, I'm more intrigued."

Olivia nodded in agreement. "Definitely not. Ghost woman doesn't know who she is dealing with."

I laughed and stepped out into the hallway. "A necromancer, the daughter of Satan, and a hunter. We make quite the team."

On our way downstairs, we stopped by our room to drop off the folder and flash drive. Then we were off to ask the desk clerk about the woman who died in 1961. The one in the articles we found in Annette's room, not the moody dark-haired woman, assuming they weren't the same. I'd ask the ghost myself if I thought she'd actually talk to me, but both times I'd tried she'd disappeared.

The lobby was empty since it was lunchtime, so that gave us some time to ask questions. A place this old had to have stories and legends. The great hall of the castle was a large, open room that had served as a gathering place for the laird and his guests. The walls were lined with tapestries, and I could easily imagine the floor covered in rush matting. A large fireplace dominated one end of the room, and there were several tables and chairs scattered around, empty this time of day, but this morning they'd been full of patrons. The castle cat, a black girl who loved getting belly rubs, was stretched in a chair in front of one of the large windows, soaking in the sunshine.

The hall was lit by oil lamps converted to electric and electric candles, and a large chandelier hung from the ceiling. They were made to flicker, and at night gave the impression they were still oil- and wax-based. The great hall was the most impressive room in the castle.

The desk clerk, an older woman with graying hair, looked up from her computer screen when we approached. "Can I help you?" she asked with a forced smile. I couldn't tell if she was annoyed by the interruption or if her mood was from something else entirely. She definitely didn't have the easy manner of Niko. I wished he was here now.

"Yes, we were wondering if you could tell us about the woman who died here in 1961," I said, giving her my brightest smile. No need to irritate her further by being standoffish.

The desk clerk furrowed her brow. "That was a long time ago. I wasn't even born then."

But she had heard about it from somewhere. There was a glint in her eyes. She knew something.

Drew leaned on the counter and flashed his most charming smile. That devil. "Do you know if anyone here remembers what happened? We're just curious, after the terrible events of last night."

"Looking for good ghost stories, if you know what we mean," Olivia added. She also flashed a winning smile. I didn't have that same sort of charm about me. But I could raise a whole graveyard to my aid if I needed to, so what did I need with charm?

"I can ask the owner. He might remember. Just a moment." The desk clerk got up from her chair and walked to the back office, through a door behind the desk. I really hadn't expected the owner to be here, though I couldn't really say why. She returned a few moments later with an older man who looked like he should have retired a few years ago. He was stooped and wrinkled, with a face that looked as though it had been carved out of an ancient tree trunk. His hair was thin and wispy, and his clothes hung loosely on his frame. He walked slowly and carefully, as though he was afraid of falling.

Despite all of this, he still managed to have a twinkle in his eye as he peered at us through thick glasses. "I'm Peter Tarkin, owner of Andarsan Castle. What can I do for you?"

I repeated our question, and he furrowed his brow, thinking. "Oh, yes, I remember that story. Back then, the Andarsan family still lived here. It was before I lived here. The woman in the photo," he tapped the photocopied picture Drew had set on the counter, "was the children's governess. Two days before Halloween, she took a nasty fall down the stairs and broke her neck. The family sold the place shortly after. Their oldest son became heir to it all. He took on the responsibility of his younger siblings." He shrugged. "I always figured they couldn't stand the stain of death. Or maybe they needed the money."

"Did they ever find out what caused her to fall?" I asked.

The man shook his head as he peered down at the photo. "No. It was ruled an accident. But there were always rumors that she'd been pushed."

I glanced from Drew to Olivia. This was definitely getting interesting. I had to know what those rumors were. If this woman was the ghost of the dead governess, she wasn't staying around because she'd died in an accident. No doubt there was something far more nefarious going on.

Then the man added, "Every year since then, on the anniversary of her death, her ghost has been seen walking around the castle. There was also talk that people felt her presence around the stairs where she died."

"Where Annette was found," I said softly, not meaning for him to hear me. But he did. Oops.

"Yes. There have been incidents where women have fallen and claimed they were pushed, but no one was around to corroborate their stories. No one has died from those accidents." He hung his head. "Until now."

We exchanged a look. Oh, yeah. We were all thinking the same thing. Annette's death was no coincidence. It was no accident. She'd been *murdered.* The question was whether or not her murderer was alive.

"Thank you for your time," I said and shook Peter's hand. "If you think of anything else, my husband, Drew, is helping the police with the investigation."

"I will let you know." Peter's eyes twinkled again before he turned to go back to the office.

"Oh, here," the clerk said. She'd stood to the side while we'd talked, listening and observing. "Don't forget the flyer for our annual Halloween ball. It's an event you definitely don't want to miss." She held out a stack of flyers, so I grabbed one to take back to our room with us. Who knew if we'd have time to go with all this going on?

CHAPTER SIX

I browsed the Halloween flyer as I walked up the stairs, but my mind was all on the case. I couldn't focus on the details of their Halloween ball. "So, it sounds like we have a murder mystery on our hands," I said as I sat down on the bed in our room. I had a couple of murder cases under my belt but, obviously, Drew had more experience than me. Olivia was all in, no matter what. She was always up for a good investigation. I could count on her.

Between the three of us, we could solve this case. The supernatural side of it. I was half convinced there wasn't a human bad guy behind any of it.

Drew nodded. "It certainly does. I'd rather us solve this than the humans."

"For sure. It sounds like there is a ghost pushing

people down the stairs." She had the same thoughts I had. Olivia took a seat at the desk in front of my laptop. Then she picked up the room service menu. "We should order lunch."

Right on cue, my stomach growled, reminding me we all skipped breakfast. "Food sounds good. While we eat, we could dig more into Annette's research of the castle. Maybe she was on the same track we were."

"And maybe that's why she got pushed down the stairs," Drew said darkly.

Neither of us had any reply to that. He was right. In all likelihood, we were in danger by investigating.

Drew and I gave Olivia our order. We had the menu memorized. She took a few minutes to pick something before she called it in. Then she turned to Drew. "Can I have the flash drive? Might as well see what was on Annette's computer."

He handed her the little thumb drive and she plugged it into my laptop. I moved to the other side of the bed so I could look over Olivia's shoulder. The desk was close enough that I could just see. Drew scooted closer to me.

We spent the entire twenty minutes it took for our lunch to arrive looking through the computer files. There wasn't much information about the castle or the ghost on her computer. It was more the fiction part of her book. "We'll have to read the actual manuscript," I said. "She might've used her theories in it."

As we ate, I thumbed through the folder with all of Annette's research. She'd scrawled notes all over the place, but it seemed likely she had no idea about the supernatural aspect. She thought she was dealing with a serial killer. And her book looked like it was going to be a contemporary, not a paranormal. She'd done the research but hadn't gotten there yet. Or the ghosts hadn't revealed themselves to her.

Munching on a delicious sweet potato fry, I picked up a news article I hadn't noticed before. The article was dated two days after the one about the governess who'd tragically fallen to her death. The laird had killed his wife and then himself in their room right after the governess died in the sixties.

I scanned through the article a few times before turning my attention to the photo to the left of the article. Holy ghoul snot! It was him. The guy, the one who'd been crying over Annette's body. The one who'd been sad in the dining room. He was the laird who'd killed his wife and then himself. And beside him in the photo was none other than the dark-haired woman who'd appeared to Drew and me the night before, asking for help. The lady with the party dress.

Well, well, well. It was all coming together, wasn't it?

"Drew, look at this," I said, handing him the article. With my hands freed up, I took advantage to take a few bites of my huge and delicious sausage.

He read through it quickly before setting it down with his eyebrows raised. "The plot thickens."

Olivia picked it up and began skimming the article, making little chirpy noises of agreement deep in her throat.

I nodded. "For sure. We should talk to the owner again and see if he knows anything about this." Surely, he had. Why hadn't he told us about it? This was absolutely related.

We finished our lunch and then made our way back down to the lobby. The owner was still at the front desk, this time without the cranky woman, and he greeted us with a smile.

"Is there anything else I can help you with?" he asked.

"We were just wondering if you could tell us more about the couple who died in the castle two days after the governess died," I said. "The man in particular. He would've been the laird?"

The owner's smile faded. "That certainly was a tragic incident. We don't like to talk about it too much because it happened in one of our rooms."

"We understand," Drew said. "But we're curious about how it all went down. Do you know which room it was?"

The owner hesitated for a moment before answering. I didn't miss that twinkle in his eye. He thought this was funny. What an imp. "It was the room you're currently staying in."

A chill ran down my spine. We'd been sleeping in the same room where two people died.

Eh, well. It wasn't that shocking. Not to a necromancer. Death was part of life, most definitely for me.

"Thank you for your time," Drew said as we turned to leave. "If you think of anything else, please. Let us know."

"You're welcome," the owner replied. "And I hope you enjoy the rest of your stay." His voice had gone back to that customer service lilt. All business.

As we walked away, I couldn't help but feel like we were being watched. I scanned the lobby, the giant pictures in their gilded frames, and the tapestries that probably hid a dozen secret passages. The fireplace and the tables. As we walked toward the stairs, I spotted a few ghosts lurking around, but they weren't the source of my feeling. They'd been here pretty much nonstop.

"While we're down here, let's mingle with the other guests. I want to see if anyone has heard any stories about the castle," I asked. Something was just bugging me. I had to figure out what it was.

Drew linked his fingers with mine. "Good idea."

CHAPTER SEVEN

"**W**hat do you think?" Olivia asked as we stepped into the dining room. Lunch was almost over, and people milled about. Some at the tables and some moving toward the great hall. "Split up?"

Drew and I nodded. "We'll go this way." I pointed toward the dining room.

"Okay. I'll head toward the fireplace." Olivia went off to find guests to mingle with to dig up any information she could.

Drew and I walked around the dining room until we found a small group of people who didn't look like they'd hiss at us if we intruded.

"So," I said conspiratorially. "Have you guys heard about the castle curse?" We wanted to know if anyone had seen anything or knew anything that would help. The best way to do that was gossip.

This little group of guests was more than happy to talk about the curse of the castle. "Oh, yeah." A woman nodded her head sagely. "It's been a rumor in this area since I was a little girl." She looked to be in her sixties or seventies, so it made sense.

"Did you grow up around here?" Drew asked.

"I did. I'm back visiting family, and they don't have room for me to stay there. I'd always wanted to stay in the castle as a child, so I figured why not stay here instead of the small inn in town?"

"I didn't grow up here, but someone at the pub in town told me all about it." A man leaned forward, looking way more excited than scared at the prospect of a ghost. "I keep trying to see one of the spirits, but as far as I can tell, this place isn't haunted." He leaned back and puffed up a bit. "I'm a bit clairvoyant, you know. If there were ghosts here, I'd feel them."

The rest of the crowd seemed properly impressed at his declaration. Drew and I exchanged an amused glance, then nodded along with the crowd, seeming to agree that the place must not be haunted.

It seemed that everyone had heard the stories

and most believed them. The most popular rumor amongst the people we talked to in the dining room was that anyone who died in the castle was doomed to haunt it forever.

I wasn't sure why the ghosts were all here, but it wasn't due to a curse. I would've felt the dark magic that powered a curse, which I didn't. It was a coincidence, or they just liked hanging out here. The only sure way to ask them was to give them power, but they, for the most part, steered clear of me. And I wasn't about to attempt the massive power surge I'd need to go into the Inbetween to talk to them properly.

As long as they weren't bothering anyone, it wasn't my or Drew's responsibility to do anything with them. The dark-haired woman and the man, on the other hand, we had to do something with because it was likely they were behind Annette's death and the accidents guests had been having on the stairs over the years. Those people who had fallen down the stairs were extremely lucky they hadn't broken their necks.

We chatted a little longer with the dining room guests before leaving to go back to our room, looking for Olivia in the front room to let her know we were headed up, but she didn't seem to be in there.

"Let's go up," Drew said. "I want to see if there's anything else in the folder that we might have missed."

"Okay. I can start reading her book, too."

When we got to our room, we found Olivia waiting for us.

"Find anything?" Drew asked her.

She shook her head and plopped back on the bed. "No, not really. Just rumors and suppositions. Nothing more informative than what the owner told us." She sat back up. "But I *did* overhear a few people talking about something strange that's been going on lately."

"What is it?" I asked and stretched out beside her on the bed. I had to find out where they got their mattresses. This one was heavenly.

"Some of the guests have been complaining about things moving in their rooms," she replied. "Like their clothes or shoes."

I laughed. "I'd rather have things moved around instead of being pushed down the stairs." Sounded like typical ghost activity. Too bad the fella we'd talked to hadn't had any of his stuff moved. That would've made his whole week. Probably his whole life.

Olivia snorted. "Me too, but these are humans

who aren't used to dealing with the strange and undead like we are."

Olivia yawned and got up, shuffling toward the portal in the mirror on the wall. "I'm going to take a little nap on your bed at home. Sam's kept me up late at night. I'll see you two later."

That portal Luci created sure was handy to have. "Okay," I said. "If we're not here, we'll be down in the lobby."

She went through, but then stuck her head back into Scotland. "Hey, if you hear anything, text me. I'll come back."

When Olivia was gone and the mirror returned to looking like a mirror instead of a shimmering wave of magic, Drew said, "That portal is handy. We won't need to fly home."

I grinned at him. "I was thinking the same thing. We should cancel our flight and see if we can get a refund or apply the points toward another trip."

He chuckled as he wrapped an arm around my waist and pulled me to him. I ended up falling on top of him, which was exactly what he'd intended for me to do. Straddling his hips, I wiggled my brows. "What do you want to do now?"

With a shift move, he flipped me onto my back. "I have a few things in mind."

Then he kissed me. Oh, yeah. I *so* liked where this was going.

It was early evening when Olivia stepped through the portal. "You could get whiplash from the time difference."

No joke. I did a quick calculation in my head. It was early afternoon in Maine. Sam would be asleep. Olivia would've had to have gotten up really early to be here with us this morning. No wonder she'd wanted to go back for a nap. "You ready for dinner?"

"Yep. I'm starving." Olivia grinned and headed to the door. "This place is amazing." She was not wrong. Even the doors were large, heavy wood, and obviously ancient. Everything about the castle was impressive.

When we got to the restaurant, we sat with some of the guests we'd met earlier in the day. They were in the middle of talking about leaving early.

"I'm not leaving," one woman with a bouffant hairdo said as she smacked the table. "I paid good money for this vacation and I'm going to enjoy it come hell or high water."

"I don't know," another woman said. "I keep

thinking I see things out of the corner of my eye." She shivered. "It's freaking me out."

"It's just your imagination," the first woman said. "There's nothing here that can hurt you."

Olivia and I didn't dare look at each other. We would've burst out laughing. Then the jig would've really been up.

It was then I spotted the owner walking towards us. Nudging Olivia, I nodded his way, which pulled Drew's attention that way, too.

Peter had a worried look on his face. When he reached our table, he spoke directly to Drew and me. "Can I speak with you for a moment?" he asked.

"Sure," Drew said and he and I got up and followed Peter—slowly, he was about a hundred—to a sitting area near the kitchen. Olivia looked like she'd swallowed a frog, not going with us. I didn't know why she'd stayed behind. She could've come with us.

Even here, which appeared to be more of an employee area, felt like I was sitting in some historic spot.

The area was decorated with dark, heavy furniture and had an enormous fireplace. A giant portrait of a woman in a white dress with her dark hair pulled back in a tight bun hung over the mantle. She had a stern look on her face, and she looked like she was staring right at me.

Creepy much?

We took a seat, Drew and I crammed onto the loveseat while Peter sat in the armchair in front of us. The fire crackled merrily, keeping the room toasty warm against the brisk October Scottish weather. Peter glanced around before focusing on us. "I take it you *are* investigating the hauntings?"

I glanced at Drew, wondering if Peter somehow knew we weren't human. Was Peter a bit supernatural himself? Drew didn't look at me as he answered the question. "We are now, yes."

The poor man leaned forward with wide eyes and whispered, "Are you hunters?"

I snorted out loud and quickly covered it with a fake coughing fit. But my dear husband said, "Yes, but we really did come here for our honeymoon. Now that we know Annette's death was caused by a ghost, we can't just ignore it."

The owner nodded. "I understand." He paused and we waited. He obviously had something he wanted to share. Finally, he said, "I was a boy when it happened, but I've never forgotten. As if the people here would let any of us forget. The rumor was that the laird of the castle was having an affair with his children's governess. She's the one who fell down the stairs. Everyone always assumed the wife did it but there was no way to prove it way back then." He shrugged. "The sixties didn't exactly have big-time forensics. Then, two days later, the laird killed his wife and himself. Their eldest son, who was of age, quickly sold the estate, having no desire to stay in the castle his parents died in. The new owners immediately started using it as a destination hotel." He sucked in a deep breath. " I got a job here as soon as I was old enough, as did many people in the village. The castle is the largest employer in the area, even still."

I looked around. It made sense that it would take an enormous staff to maintain this place.

"I lived on-site and saved every penny of my paychecks. By the time they were ready to sell, when I was in my 40s, I had enough for the down payment."

"What about the women falling down the stairs?" I asked.

"It happens every ten years on the anniversary of the governess's death. The last time, before Annette's death, the hotel was closed for renovations. We'd actually planned it that way, to hopefully keep anyone from falling." He shook his head regretfully.

"But somehow a young woman wandered into the castle while it was locked up tight and fell down the stairs." The owner looked into the fire for a moment, then continued. "We've done seances, called so-called ghost hunters, but nothing has worked. Every decade, another young woman falls down the stairs."

"We'll figure it out and solve the mystery," I said. "It's what we do."

Drew added, "If there is any more information you can give us, that will help."

Peter took out one of his business cards and wrote down the Laird's name, his wife's, and the governess's. Malcolm, Nora, and Holly. "That's all I know about them."

"It's a start. Thank you." I took the card and tucked it into my pants pocket.

Then Drew and I returned to the table. Olivia had turned the conversation around while we were talking to Peter. The group was laughing and chatting about their adventures since staying at The Andarsan. My besty stared at me with questions in her eyes, but I couldn't exactly fill her in now. She'd have to wait till after dinner. No doubt it was going to kill her to wait. I giggled and took a sip of my water. Poor Olivia.

CHAPTER EIGHT

"What if we do our own seance?" I asked, moving my gaze from Drew to Olivia. We'd just returned from dinner and now that we were alone in our room—the room where the Laird and his wife had died. I'd filled Olivia in on the owner's story as we walked back to our room.

Olivia nodded quietly, a thin smile on her lips. She was loving every minute of this. I hated to remind her this wasn't all fun and games. Someone had *died*.

Drew scratched the back of his neck and lifted one shoulder. "I don't see how it could hurt," he said. "We've done them before."

Of course, there were ways it could hurt, hurt a lot, but I was betting on my necro powers to keep the spirits from harming us or anyone else. I hoped. They were still super wonky. At least now we knew why. My powers had been so strong before because I was the last female descendant on both sides of my family. But now that my son's girlfriend was pregnant with a baby girl. That had to be what was causing my powers to only work when they wanted to. My mother had told me that when she was pregnant with me, she had problems with her powers as well. I never did with Wallie, but I didn't really use my powers when I was pregnant with him. I'd still been denying my abilities at that point.

"Shouldn't we wait for dark?" Olivia asked as I conjured a few candles, matches, and some salt, happy my malfunctioning powers allowed me to do this much.

"Nah, that's not necessary. It's possible that doing them during the witching hour would make them stronger, but there's a large debate about when the witching hour actually is, so, meh." I shrugged.

We needed a larger space to work, so I had Drew move the bed to the side, which ended up being impossible. The bed was a *gigantic* solid four-poster and as strong as Drew was, even with his supernatural hunter strength, there was no moving it on his own. Olivia wiggled her fingers, the bed rose up, drifted off to the side, and sat gently back down on the ground.

I poured salt into a large circle while Olivia placed the candles around the salt line and lit them.

We sat outside the salt circle, and I held out my hands. "I want the ghosts contained in the circle, so don't let go."

Drew and I took Olivia's hands, each of us having to lean a bit to reach. The air felt charged, but it was hard to tell if that was me or the ghosts.

Tension knotted my neck as I fed my power into the circle. A buzz of energy forced me to open my eyes, and a thick silver rope of light wrapped around Olivia's and my hands, drawing us together in a solid barrier. Light from the candles flickered as our circle snapped together. Now the silver rope of light ran down all of our arms and hands.

Drew sucked in a breath. As a hunter, he was bred to hate this sort of thing.

I loved it.

His magic started to rebel against mine and Olivia's, so I waited. It needed time to be comfortable with this, and we had time to be patient. Drew's magic was part of mine, ever since we'd bonded, just as mine was part of his now. However, Olivia's magic was a mix of fae and underworld power, and Drew had never connected with her magic before.

It was freaking him and his magic out.

"Drew?" I arched a brow at him. He had to get himself together.

"I got it." He closed his eyes and took deep, even breaths. I could sense his magic calming down, listening to whatever he was telling it. Or maybe as his heart rate slowed and he got himself under control, the magic followed suit. Sometimes I talked to mine, and sometimes it just did what I wanted. It was a topic of conversation I should bring up another time. It would make for an interesting conversation at the next coven meeting.

Drew smiled shakily. "I'm good now."

Olivia watched us with a worried expression. I quickly explained. "Hunter magic doesn't play well with darker powers. And let's face it. Half of your magic is as dark as it comes."

She snickered and nodded. "True."

We sat quietly for a few minutes to ground ourselves and clear our minds. Then I took the lead by pushing out my necro power, which seemed to be working for the moment. When the salt circle was full of my power, boosted by Olivia's and Drew's, I spoke, also lacing my words with magic. "Malcolm Andarsan, show yourself."

We waited in calm silence for a few minutes. Nothing happened. Talk about anticlimactic.

"Is there anyone here with us?" Olivia asked in a soft voice.

We waited for a few more minutes, then I tried again with a little more magic, really cramming the circle full. This castle was chock full of ghosts. What the heck? There was no response.

"Maybe this isn't going to work," Drew said, sounding doubtful.

I was about to agree when the candles flickered and went out. A few seconds later the candles lit on their own and inside the circle was a ghost. It wasn't Malcolm Andarsan, but this ghost was definitely Scottish and dressed in nothing but a kilt. He locked eyes with me, then Olivia laughed like someone had told him a really good joke, then flipped his kilt up, flashing us his private bits.

Trust me, ghost bits weren't as exciting as the real thing. Or maybe just *this* ghost's bits weren't.

Just then, a noise came from the other side of the room, near the bathroom. It sounded like someone was crying. We all turned to look but there was nothing there. When we looked back, the flasher ghost was gone.

"Did you hear that?" I whispered. Why did this freak me out so much? This was nothing new or strange for me.

Drew and Olivia both nodded their heads, Olivia with wide, startled eyes. We sat in silence for a few more minutes, but we didn't hear the crying again.

"Well, that was weird," Drew said. Then he shot up to his feet and started waving his arms around like he was fighting off an invisible attacker. He bobbed and weaved, grunting. "Help me," he said as he flailed.

"Holy crap, he's possessed!" Olivia scrambled to her feet, and I followed suit, fear bubbling up my throat.

I grabbed Drew's hand, but the invisible force still held onto him with a vice-like grip. I tried to pull back but now he had a hold of me. I couldn't get him to release my fingers.

"Drew, let go of my hand so I can break the connection," I said, ready to fight the ghost or spirit or whatever the heck it was. I gathered my powers, ready to blast this ghost into oblivion.

Drew tried to shake his head, but he was still unable to break the ghost's hold on him. "Help!" He looked seriously freaked out, my big strong hunter. I had to help him!

Tears pricked my eyes as I scrambled to figure out what I could do. "Drew, please. I don't want to hurt you."

Drew nodded his head, then after a deep breath, he let go of my hand. At that moment, the invisible force released him. Drew fell to his knees and started gasping for air.

"Get him some water," I said to Olivia while I searched Drew's body for injuries. Could the ghost have bodily harmed him?

Probably. They could be nasty.

Olivia darted into the bathroom as I used my healing powers to feel if he was injured. Besides a racing heart, I didn't think he was.

A moment later the water turned on, then Olivia returned with a glass and put it to Drew's lips. He gulped down the entire glass. "Are you okay?" she asked, leaning over him.

Drew nodded his head. "That was not fun."

I helped him to his feet while monitoring his emotions through our bond. "Are you sure you're okay?"

Drew nodded but his teal eyes looked a little

glazed over. He was emotionally rung out but physically fine.

Olivia and I helped Drew over to the bed so he could sit on it. I walked to the salt circle and used my magic to gather it up in a small cyclone, then directed it to the trash can. One of my little parlor tricks that were so handy. With a wave of my hand, the candles went out.

Just then we heard a dull thumping noise. "What now?" I asked, more than exasperated.

CHAPTER NINE

Ah! There it was again. The hollow thump, thump, thump was coming from inside our wall. What in the world could be in there? I waved at Olivia and pointed at the wall beside the tapestry. She nodded and came closer. "I already checked behind there for a hidden passage," she whispered.

Drew scoffed. "I looked there the first day."

At least it wasn't another ghost ready to possess one of us. Well, it could've been, but I doubted it since the banging sounded like something or someone, possibly, was stuck in the wall. Ghosts could've just gone through it.

Drew, Olivia, and I pushed against the wall where the noise was coming from, poking and prodding on the crown molding, and the baseboards, and tugging on the light sconces. "It would be something old, original to the house," Olivia said. "The secret entrance won't be in a modern electric light.

I eyeballed the fireplace mantle across the room. "Possibly it's not something close?" I hurried over and began prodding away at the intricately carved mantle.

Sure enough, the inner circle of a little flower depressed with just a little bit of pressure. After a couple of seconds, a secret door popped open on the other side of the exit door, several feet away from where we'd been searching.

A stale, dank musty smell, like an airless, damp basement, came with it. We peered into the dark, creepy passage, which went in the direction of the original thumps we'd heard.

I shrieked when something came rushing toward us, and everyone jumped back as Lucy-Fur and Snoozer came running out.

"We've been yelling for you for hours!" Lucy said in almost a growl.

I gaped at my incredibly spoiled, cute-but-so-bad cats. "How in all the heavens did you get in there?"

Lucy tossed her snow-white head back haughtily. "We came through the portal earlier, when you weren't here and decided to have a nap on that amazing bed while we waited.

I felt the urge for a moment of private time, so I went looking for a litter box and found a passage." She glared at Snoozer. "I don't know how he opened it, but I know it was him."

"Was he up on the mantle?" Drew asked.

Snoozer licked his paw delicately. He loved being up high.

"Yes," Lucy said darkly. "Right after I went into the passage, he ran in behind me. Somehow the door shut behind us, and we were stuck."

"What did you find?" I asked. "Where does it go?"

Lucy gave me a disdainful look. "Do I look stupid to you? Do I look like a complete idiot? Do you think for one second that I would stray away from the opening we came in? The moment we went any further down the passage we would've ended up getting lost." She huffed, and it sounded suspiciously like a hiss. "We stayed right by the door until we heard you lot come back from wherever you'd been enjoying yourselves." Man, her voice *dripped* with venom.

"Well, heck. I want to see where it goes!" Olivia jumped up and down on the balls of her feet.

We followed the passage using the lights from our cell phones and found ourselves in a room with cobwebs draping from the ceiling and dust everywhere. It was so quiet that I could hear my own heart beating.

Olivia conjured an energy ball to light up the room.

"Oh, gosh." It was awesome. I quickly realized that the room was a secret reading room. Everything had been carefully put in place. There was a small lounge with a quilt on it. Nearby, in a wooden case near a window, a stack of books was neatly piled from top to bottom.

To the left of the lounger was a round table. On it, there was a candlestick in the center and an old-fashioned matchbox nearby. Next to the candlestick was a stack of folded papers with a quill and an inkwell. The corners were curled with age and the paper was yellowed.

We searched the room for any clues about who the late Laird Andarsan and his wife had been. What sort of people were they? Had they been kind or cruel, rash or calm? We knew nothing.

After a few minutes, Olivia muttered, "I think I found something." She was splayed out on the floor where she'd been checking floorboards. Grinning from ear to ear, she reached down and lifted a loose floorboard. She reached underneath and pulled out an old, leather-bound book. Its spine was worn from use, but the pages were still in good shape.

"What is it?" I asked, hurrying over to crouch beside her on the floor.

"I think it's an old journal," she said, holding it up for me to see. "Maybe there's something in here that can help us."

I took the journal from her and started flipping through it.

It was Nora Andarsan's diary. Olivia and I sat back, and she conjured another orb to hover.

The woman's handwriting was neat and so easy to read. We skimmed, mainly looking at dates and a few sentences per page. It seemed like it covered her turmoil leading up to the deaths and included the day she shoved the governess down the stairs. The last entry was on October 30, 1961. She'd been getting ready for the Halloween ball and the entry talked about being excited about her dress and that her husband was finally her own. She even described it. "That dress is the one she's wearing to this day," I whispered. "The one her ghostly body adorns." I spoke in a spooky voice and dissolved into giggles.

Once I composed myself, Olivia looked at me with wide eyes.

"That's the day they died," she said, in a low tone.

I nodded, suddenly feeling sad, my giggles disappearing, which was crazy because Nora had killed her husband's mistress and gotten away with it. Did she deserve to die for her crime? Perhaps. Her husband had clearly thought so.

I flipped to the last page, hoping for some sort of explanation, but there was none. No more entries past that night. "That's the last one." It seemed indecent to raise my voice in here, so I kept my tone low.

"Cause she was dead," Drew said ironically. He was studying the books on the shelves.

"Drew," I hissed. "Be respectful."

An answering chuckle was all I got.

Maybe this journal was the key to helping the ghosts move on. But first, we needed to find out why they were still stuck at the castle. What was keeping them here? And not just the three involved with this intrigue. Why was this a hotspot for ghost activity in general?

If I remembered correctly, one of the ghosts on the ghost train had told me there were certain places ghosts just enjoyed hanging out. Maybe this was one. Heck if I knew.

I studied the journal again, flipping through the pages until I came to an entry from the day before the Halloween ball. There was something else here. Scrawled in the margins of the page, hidden under layers of yellowed ink and etchings, were two words: stuck forever. The word forever was underlined several times, and the ink was weird.

Geeeeeez. "Is that blood?" I whispered, pointing to the words.

Olivia nodded with a shiver. "This place is spooky."

Had Nora bound her husband and his mistress to this castle so they would be forced to relive their deaths over and over again for all of eternity? How had she done it? Had she cast some sort of dark magic spell before her death? The other guests at the castle had mentioned a curse. Was that what they had meant? Or were there secrets buried deep in Andarsan Castle that only the family knew about?

One thing was for sure—our investigation into this mystery would keep us occupied for some time as we desperately searched for answers from beyond the grave.

"Let's get out of here," I said as I took one last look around at all of the old books and artifacts in the secret room.

"As spooky as it is," Olivia said. "This room is so cool. I gotta ask Luci if there are secret passages in his house."

I snorted as I led Drew and Olivia back through the passage. "Knowing your father, there are some that lead to places or rooms that you don't want to see."

"Eww." She drew out the word. "Gross, I bet you're right. I'll definitely *ask* before I go exploring."

We turned right, and I had a vague feeling that we took a wrong turn. My feeling was cemented when we came to a set of stairs going down. We had taken a wrong turn, dang it. I definitely didn't remember there being stairs on our way into the secret reading room. That wasn't the sort of thing I'd forget.

As we came to the bottom of the stairwell, we emerged into the lobby right next to the large fireplace. "This is interesting." As busy as the lobby was, nobody seemed to notice our emergence from nowhere.

"Yep," Drew agreed.

Olivia nodded.

As we made our way through the lobby to the elevators, goosebumps rose on my arms and shivers danced down my spine as if Nora herself was watching me from beyond her grave.

Which was likely, since I now knew she was the dark-haired ghost who'd woken me up to help. But why would she have asked us to help when she was the one who'd trapped Malcolm and Holly there? It made no sense. Either she wanted them freed or she didn't. Maybe she'd just had a major afterlife change of heart.

Despite how unsettled I felt, we were determined to find out what happened to Malcolm Andarsan and his lover, Holly, so they could finally rest in peace once again. Maybe we'd get lucky and find a way to help Nora find some peace, too.

If there was anything left behind by them in this castle or even clues about their deaths elsewhere, then it was our mission to unearth those secrets for good and put their souls to rest forever.

10

OLIVIA

I woke with a start like someone had doused me with water. What happened? Blinking rapidly, I waited for my eyesight to catch up with my brain as I checked my surroundings. No wonder it was hard for me to get my bearings. I was no longer in Ava and Drew's bedroom where I'd fallen asleep. I'd stumbled through the portal and collapsed on their bed to get a few hours' sleep. Going back and forth was messing with me, even with Sammie busy with his grandmother Phira and Sam busy with Wade planning the bar. Just the time difference was getting to me. It had still been early evening when I'd fallen asleep back in Maine.

Now I was standing at the top of a set of stairs, with just a sliver of moonlight coming through a window to light the way. Panicked, I turned to rush back to their room when I felt a presence behind me. It did not feel friendly, either.

I sensed her before I saw her. The hairs on my neck lifted, and the feeling of being watched grew stronger.

"Go! And never return!" shouted an angry voice in front of me. A dark-haired woman in a ballgown stared down at me. Her eyes were so dark they looked black, and her face was contorted with rage. She floated several inches off the ground. "You never belonged here!" she shrieked, then she shoved me down the stairs.

I had no time to brace myself for the fall. Pain exploded in my ankles and shoulders as I tumbled down the staircase. It happened so fast, but I had to get out of there.

Before I hit the ground, I teleported myself without really thinking about where I was going. I needed a safe place to land. Like a trampoline. My body disappeared from the castle and reappeared on a trampoline in the backyard of my childhood home. I bounced on the trampoline and held myself still, trying to get the creaking of the old thing to stop. Crap. I couldn't be there. If my *very* human, adopted parents had seen me appear out of thin air, I wasn't sure how they'd react. I certainly couldn't explain myself.

Rolling off of the trampoline, I disappeared underneath it before I quickly teleported myself back into Scotland and Ava and Drew's room.

I stumbled to Ava and Drew's big comfy bed, still clutching my shoulder. My whole body ached, but I was afraid my shoulder was bruised or jammed. It definitely didn't feel good. "Ava, Drew. Wake up!" I cried. Snoozer jumped off the bed and ran under it with a yowl.

Lucy did it with a, "What the fu—"

"What's wrong?" Ava asked, cutting the cranky cat off, her sleepiness quickly forgotten. She rolled out of bed and rushed to me, grabbing my elbow, thankfully the one on my arm that wasn't currently throbbing.

"Someone pushed me down the stairs!" I explained. "It was the ghost, the one you described in the ball gown. Nora."

"Are you sure?" Drew asked, looking just as worried as Ava. He pulled on a dressing gown and helped Ava get me to the bed.

"Positive," I said. "She screamed at me to go away and never come back. Then she hauled off and shoved me."

"Well, we aren't leaving until we find out how to stop her from pushing other women down the stairs," Ava said, moving closer to me. "This will sting a bit."

I opened my mouth to ask her what she was doing when her cool hand landed gently on the bruised, tender spot on my shoulder. A tingle of something warm and soft spread slowly through me as she pushed her healing magic into me. Soon all my aches vanished.

"That's better. Thanks," I said, then asked, "I thought she wanted our help. What gives?"

"Maybe she does," Ava said. "Maybe she can't stop her mood swings. Remember how Phira was an evil black blob in the Inbetween? She was stuck somewhere she didn't belong and had lost her daughter."

I had never considered that, but it made sense. Phira's corrupted father had punished her for falling in love with Luci. Phira had been sent to the Inbetween, which was sort of a hell dimension for witches. Human ghosts also spent a lot of time there. Fae ghosts were not ever meant to go there. Phira's pain and the magic from the Inbetween had turned her into this massive evil blob of black slime. It wasn't until my blood had touched her that she turned back to herself—a fae princess, my biological mother, and a wonderful person.

"Being stuck in the castle is making Nora's ghost go crazy."

Ava nodded. "That's my working theory."

"We won't be scared off that easily," Drew said with a smirk before leaning over and stroking Ava's cheek with the back of his hand. She closed her eyes and relaxed, leaning into his touch like a cat who had just discovered where her bowl of catnip was kept.

Ah, newlyweds. My chest tightened. I missed Sam. I missed the ease we'd had with one another before.

Since he'd become a vampire, our schedules had been off. When he was awake, he couldn't stay away from me for too long. He clung. It was unhealthy to go on as we had been. I had to figure out how to fix that. Fix us. These last few nights with him focused on the bar had been great, but almost too much distance. I'd barely seen him at all. We had to find a nice in-between. A compromise. Middle ground.

But I couldn't do that right at this moment, so I focused on our little ghostly mystery. This was fun. We should start solving mysteries like this more often.

"There's not much we can do right now. It's

almost sunrise." Ava groaned. She'd never been an early riser.

I patted her hand sympathetically. "We can go back to sleep for a bit, then go into town tomorrow to see what we can dig up about the Andarsans. Surely someone remembers something important."

Ava crawled back under the covers. "Sounds good to me."

I moved to the portal in the mirror and stepped through to Ava and Drew's bedroom in Maine. Winston gave the floorboards under my feet a little shake in greeting. "Hi, Winston." At least he'd stopped treating me like the black sheep of the family. Six months ago if I'd stepped into the house while Ava and Drew were gone, he would've completely revolted.

Staring at the bed, I debated whether or not to take a little nap. Going back and forth from Scotland to Maine was really screwing with my internal clock. Hmm. I wasn't sleepy. I *should've* been, but no dice.

The familiar rumble of Sam's voice echoed from downstairs. Aww. My bae, as my daughter Jess would've said.

With a smile, I turned and made my way downstairs, following my hubby's voice to the kitchen where he, Wade, and Luci sat going over plans for the new vampire bar. This venture couldn't have come at a better time. It was just what he needed to find some purpose again and to help him acclimate to his fanged lifestyle.

I sat in his lap, and he curled his arms around me, hugging me close while burying his nose into my neck. "I've missed your scent," he whispered.

"I've missed us." I laid my head on his shoulder with a sigh.

"We'll fix it," he said. "We'll get through it. Every marriage goes through ups and downs."

I agreed wholeheartedly and settled in to listen to them talk about location options and plans for the building. Sam seemed at peace and happy for the first time since he'd been turned. That made me happier than I'd been in weeks.

It made sense that being stuck in the castle was making Nora's ghost go crazy. What didn't make sense was that it seemed like she was the one who trapped them there, to begin with.

The only thing we could do right now was try to sleep, hoping that when we woke again, we might be able to figure out some way of getting rid of her spirit once and for all. And hopefully without any of us becoming possessed again.

I sighed as I crawled back into bed with Drew and pulled the covers over us both, trying not to think about what would happen if our efforts failed. It was only a matter of time before someone else died. If Olivia hadn't had portaling powers, it could've been her, tonight.

There was nothing else I wanted more at this moment than rid the castle of Nora's ghost.

Just as I started drifting off, a familiar meow startled me awake again. Snoozer. I reached down and scratched his head. As I closed my eyes, I felt another cat jump on the bed. At first, I thought it was Lucy, but when I looked over at the chair by the balcony door, Lucy was curled up sleeping in it. She'd settled there after finally coming out from under the bed. She'd had a few choice words and phrases for Olivia as she went, too.

Um, who else was in my bed?

I sat up and raised my eyebrows as, in the moonlight coming through the balcony windows, I watched the castle cat, Nix, rubbing up against Snoozer like she was happy to meet a new friend. It was sweet. Snoozer let Nix greet him, though he seemed a little on edge. Everything remained relatively calm for a minute.

Until Lucy woke up. The moment Lucy caught sight of the castle cat, she jumped to her feet and glared bloody murder. Yes, cats can glare. I've seen it. I was seeing it right then.

With a blood-curdling cry that sounded like a woman fighting off a monster in a horror movie, Lucy leaped off of the chair and launched herself at the bed and at the castle cat. "How dare you come in here you brazen buddy!" Nix didn't speak people, but she must've understood because she began her own ear-splitting shrieks as tufts of fluff flew. The two felines, one snowy white and the other pitch black rolled around on top of Drew's legs, waking him up with his own yell.

Mindful of all the claws, I grabbed Lucy and pulled her off of the poor black cat. Snoozer was nowhere to be found. As soon as he'd heard Lucy screaming, he'd gotten the heck out of Dodge.

As gently as I could, I pushed Lucy off the bed and onto the floor, where she settled herself with a huff. "Get that bit—"

"Lucy!" I scolded.

"—that *homewrecker* out of here!"

Drew picked Nix up, carried her to the door, and put her out in the hallway. I wasn't even sure how the cat had gotten into our room, to begin with.

Just then, Olivia walked through the mirror portal.

"What's up?" She looked at the two cats, then over to us. Lucy stood glaring at Snoozer while he peeked out from underneath the desk. "Or should I ask?"

I laughed and explained about the castle cat and how she'd just jumped into bed with us.

"I took care of business," Lucy said with a shake of her tail. "That bi—"

"Lucy..." I warned again.

"That *cow* will think twice before trying to get her claws into my Snoozie again."

I finished explaining about the catfight between Nix and Lucy.

Olivia laughed. "Well, it looks like someone is feeling a little left out."

She walked over and scratched Snoozer behind his ears. He purred and crept out from under the desk to let her scratch his back.

Then Olivia turned her attention to Lucy, who was still glaring at the door where the other cat had been moments before. It was like she expected Nix to come back. Or more like wishing she would so she could finish the job. Geez, Lucy could be so dramatic.

"Poor Lucy. You had to defend your man, didn't you?" Olivia said as she picked her up. To my surprise, Lucy didn't protest too much about being picked up. When she started squirming, Olivia sat her on the bed with Snoozer.

Lucy looked at Snoozer. "You're not innocent in this."

He hunkered down in response.

Olivia smirked and looked at me. "Since we're up, let's go shopping for Halloween costumes for the ball. I had a look at the flyer, and I really want to go. Plus, maybe while we're in town we can ask around about the Andarsans and the castle."

We called for a taxi, then headed down to the lobby to wait. By the time I was in the car, squished between Drew and Olivia, I felt much better. Having a different focus besides ghosts and mysteries helped to calm my nerves. It probably didn't hurt to be out of the menacing atmosphere Nora brought to the castle. Plus, going to town to shop brought on a thrill of its own. I did love Halloween and dressing up.

We quickly found a cute little boutique shop with a massive costume section. The racks were filled with everything from biker chick outfits to superhero capes, pirate swords, and beautiful gowns for beauty queens. And everything in between.

"Ooh, look at this one." I held up a hotdog costume. It was cute and would definitely get a laugh.

"I think you should try it on," Olivia said with a grin.

"Why not?" I snagged the costume and headed into the dressing room.

A few minutes later I came out of the dressing room and did a little twirl for Olivia and Drew with my arms spread out.

Olivia laughed and then applauded. "It's perfect for you."

It was ridiculous, but fun too. At least Sammie would have gotten a kick out of it if he were here. I grinned, loving the idea of wearing such a silly costume.

Drew smirked and said, "I think it's hot."

I stared at him, trying not to burst out in a fit of laughter. Through our bond, I felt his amusement. In fact, he was barely holding it together.

"No, I think I need something a little sexier," I teased. "Let's see what they have."

Olivia laughed and rummaged through the rack, pulling out one after another outfit to try on.

After trying on a few more different looks while Drew made appropriately interested noises, we settled on a couple of vintage matching dresses. Olivia's was dark purple velvet with a rose-gold lace overlay at the waist. Mine was black and accented by silver chains at strategic places that made it look like they belonged there. We also picked up a couple of cat ears that clipped into our hair and looked a little too realistic.

Then it was Drew's turn. He opted for a kilt and tartan with a heavy sporran hanging in the front that made him look like he'd stepped out of a historical romance novel. Be still my heart. It was *extremely* difficult to keep my hands off of him.

Happy with our finds, we paid for our outfits and accessories before heading out to grab lunch at a cozy cafe nearby.

As we ate, a middle-aged woman, maybe a bit younger than me, with long black hair peppered with gray approached our table. She seemed excited to talk to us and barely waited for the waitress to leave before starting up a conversation.

"Heard you were in town looking into the Andarsan castle curse," she said with a twinkle in her eye and a thick Scottish accent. A local, for sure. "Oh, I can tell you so many stories about that place."

I glanced at Drew and Olivia before returning my attention to the woman. "How did you know that?" I asked. "It wasn't like we advertised." Maybe she'd talked to one of the guests that we'd talked to the other night.

"I'm psychic," she offered with a smile and a wave of her hand.

Sure. Why not?

"I knew you'd be coming here seeking answers. And that it's important you know Laird Andarsan's son is still alive and lives nearby."

She pulled a piece of paper out of her bag and wrote down an address. "GPS will take you right there. I hope you three can free their spirits."

I took the paper when she held it out. "You're psychic. I assume you're involved with a local coven?" That's how it was in the States. Most all witch-related paranormals belonged to the coven. It was a safety measure, really. "Why haven't you or your coven done anything about it?"

"Oh, we have." Oh, good. It was the same here. She was with a coven. "Or at least we've tried. Nora's ghost is too strong even with the power of thirteen. She blocks us out." The woman frowned and then looked out the window as if in a daze. Then she said, "I have to go." She jumped to her feet and rushed to the door, then disappeared from sight.

This was the strangest honeymoon I'd ever been on.

CHAPTER TWELVE

As we pored over historical records in the public library of the castle, my heart raced with excitement. I hated that someone had died, but Olivia's enthusiasm for solving a mystery had rubbed off on me.

We combed through old maps and documents, searching for clues about where Malcolm, Nora, and Holly might be buried. At first, we'd thought a quick internet search would provide the records, but no such luck. The last thing I wanted to do was bother the son of the laird and dredge all this up for him again, but if we didn't find some information in this library we might have to.

After hours of meticulous research and poring over ancient records, we finally found what we were looking for: a cemetery nestled deep in a forest at the edge of town, near but not on the castle's property. "They must not have wanted to bury murderers and murder victims here on the manor grounds," Olivia murmured as we looked at the cemetery map. "Bad juju and all that." Excitement mounted with every step that brought us closer to our goal.

After bundling up against the Scottish wind, we eagerly followed an overgrown path through dense underbrush towards the graveyard shrouded by looming trees. At least it was secluded. There didn't seem to be a ton of people vying to spend time at this particular graveyard.

We carefully made our way through rows upon rows of mossy gravestones, using a little discreet magic to clean them off enough to read them, until finally reaching three distinct markers bearing familiar names etched into their surfaces long ago by grieving loved ones.

"Why would they bury them side-by-side?" I asked. "That's... weird."

"And wouldn't the laird normally be in some fancy mausoleum?" Olivia looked around. "There isn't anything like that here. This graveyard is super lonely."

It didn't even have large gravestones. Just small,

rectangular ones. Most graveyards in Maine held a mixture of large and small, ornate and simple.

"We may never know," Drew said. "Those things were made sixty years ago."

"Let's raise Holly, the governess, first," I said. "She's the only ghost we haven't seen yet. Maybe she's not actually trapped in the castle but can give us some answers."

Olivia used her power to lift the dirt from the grave and cast it aside. Then my powerful friend lifted the lid of the coffin, revealing Holly's skeleton. "That's handy." I didn't have the ability to raise all that dirt, or at least I'd never tried. They generally just clawed their way out of the ground. Bit of a PITA for the poor animated skeletons. Maybe I'd try the dirt thing the next time I had to unbury someone.

I knelt by the hole and pressed my fingers against the dirt, too far away to reach the bones. I wasn't trying to climb in and out of any six-foot holes today.

I focused on Holly's body and urged my power to flow into the bones. Dirt popped and hissed, floating away from the exposed bones draped in a nice dress. Holly shifted, bones that had been dead for sixty years rising up from the coffin, held together by magic and my will.

It'd been a while since I'd dealt with an animated

skeleton. I'd forgotten how comical they were. Holly looked around wildly until her gaze fell on me. Don't ask how I knew her skeleton was looking at me. I just knew. Maybe it had something to do with living with Larry as a skeleton for as long as I had. Heavens, don't let me laugh now.

"Why am I here?" Holly asked softly. Her fear vibrated off her. "Who are you?"

"My name is Ava." I motioned to Drew and Olivia and introduced them. "This is my husband Drew and my best friend Olivia. We know what happened to you and Malcolm. We're here to help you move on."

Holly's eye holes filled with tears, and she shook her head vigorously before replying, "No! You can't! If you do, Nora will kill you too."

"We're a little too hard to kill." I didn't go into why.

"Yeah," Olivia chimed in. "You don't have to worry about us."

Once back in her ghostly form, Holly would sense what we were, probably. They always seemed to know what I was, anyway.

"Nora killed me," Holly said matter-of-factly. "And has been holding Malcolm and me in the castle ever since, forcing us to relive our deaths every ten years."

"Why?" I asked. "What does she want?"

"Revenge," Holly replied simply. "Nora is consumed by hate for me and my Malcolm. She wants us to suffer as she did."

Holly sighed and leaned against the side of her grave. "Where did they bury me?" But she kept talking before I could tell her. "Nora blames me for their failed marriage, and we shouldn't have had an affair. We were wrong. But their bond was falling apart *long* before Malcolm and I fell in love."

"How can we help you?" Olivia asked. "We need to know what she did to trap you both so we can set you and Malcolm free."

"I don't know, in this form," Holly said, glancing around as if searching for something or someone. Probably she was looking for Malcolm. "Maybe if Malcolm was with me, we could move on together."

"Hang tight," I said and went to his grave a few feet from Holly's. "Stay right there."

Olivia did the dirt thing, obviously trying to hurry. She was a little sloppy with the dirt moving but got the job done. As soon as the casket was open, I animated Malcolm's bones. He stood, wearing scraps of what looked to be a kilt. It barely hung on by threads around his waist. He looked around, and once he saw his lady love, tried to climb out of his grave.

It didn't go so well.

Drew choked back a laugh as Malcolm fell back into his grave and his arm popped off. "Seems to be a theme with skeletons we know." Larry was always losing his head back when he hadn't had flesh. Heck, sometimes it still tries to fall off.

"Oh, yeah, sorry," Olivia said after elbowing the barely composed Drew. She lifted the dirt from between their graves so they could reach one another.

The skeletons embraced, legs intertwined, and arms wrapped around each other. Without skin and... well, bodies to stop them, their bones intertwined, rib cages going inside each other. It was a few steps past disturbing.

Olivia snorted back a laugh and leaned into me to whisper, "They're boning."

I choked on my spit as I tried valiantly not to laugh, and Drew failed to cover his laugh with a cough.

They held each other for a while, long after we'd composed ourselves, their arms wrapped tightly around each other, until Malcolm finally said, "Thank you."

Their souls rose out of them, two shining white orbs that hovered a few seconds over us before dancing around our heads then shooting straight up into the sky and disappearing.

Their bones rattled down into Holly's casket, nearly perfectly lining up. "Can you adjust them?" I asked. "Let's leave their bones to rest together for all of eternity."

"Aw, I love that." Olivia beamed at me.

At the same time, Drew rolled his eyes. "There's nothing left of them in the bones," he said.

I poked him in the side while Olivia wiggled her finger and the bones shifted so they were fully together in the casket, then she shut both the full casket and the empty one.

Olivia raised her hands, and the air hummed as she willed the piles of dirt to rise up and float above the graves. With a look of concentration, Olivia attempted to shift the dirt over the holes, but she'd tried to do it all at once. Both graves, and the dirt from between them. Instead of neatly repacking the dirt, she lost her grip on her telekinesis and one pile of dirt fell on Lucy and Snoozer, who I hadn't even realized had followed us out here. I was glad the two cats were immortal ghouls, or they would have been seriously injured.

Lucy, in her dramatic fashion, screeched, and even Snoozer yowled. "I knew it!" Lucy screamed as Olivia rapidly moved the dirt again. "You hate me! You've always hated me. You want to see me suffer."

"Oh, Lucy." I picked her up and dusted her off with my own power.

Thankfully, they were both okay, just a little dirty.

When we finished putting the bones to rest, which mainly consisted of Olivia making sure the graves looked normal, repositioning the grass, and patting it all down, we turned to the third grave. Two ghosts down. One to go. I had a feeling the last one wasn't going to be nearly so easy.

CHAPTER THIRTEEN

Attempting to animate Nora's skeleton, I poured my necromancer magic into the pile of bones. It wasn't working. Darkness fell as I tried, and minutes turned into more minutes.

I closed my eyes and tried to imagine purple light flowing from my body into the bones. Breathing slowly and deeply, I sent the bones all my healing energy, but nothing happened. I tried several times more until Drew finally placed a hand on my shoulder in a silent plea to stop. "It's not my magic this time," I said. "It's actually working properly. It's as if there's an invisible barrier separating me from Nora's spirit." I couldn't call her ghost to me, no matter what I did or how hard I tried.

"What now? I thought Nora wanted us to free

her." Despite being a necromancer, I didn't know much about ghosts or why they acted the way they did.

Drew pulled out his phone. "I met a hunter once that specialized in ghosts. Blair Braden. She's retired now, but I'm sure she'll answer a couple of questions."

I didn't know hunters actually retired. Drew had, of course, but his family still called him on occasion to try to pull him back in. Hunters didn't allow their members to leave the ranks easily. Kinda like the mafia, but with a noble purpose. I had a feeling that they would try harder now that they'd met me and were starting up a paranormal liaison division. I wasn't even sure what that all entailed, but it was sure to become a headache for Drew and me at some point.

Drew dialed Blair's number and put her on speaker. She answered on the second ring. "It's never good when a Walker calls me, but *you* are supposed to be as retired as I am."

"When are any of us really retired?" Drew asked.

Blair laughed. "True. What can I do for you, Drew? Wait. Aren't you supposed to be on your honeymoon?"

"News travels fast." Drew rolled his eyes, then

said, "You're on speaker. My wife, Ava, and our friend Olivia are here."

Liv and I said, "Hi," at the same time.

"Hello." There was the sound of a male voice in the background, then Blair said, "Don't touch that. It might be cursed."

I raised a brow at Drew, and he explained. "Blair owns an antique store where she looks for cursed objects and other relics and reports them to hunter HQ. AKA Pearl."

"Ah, so she's not truly retired either," I said with a grin. Drew's grandmother had mentioned several times that hunters never retire. Many pretend they are, but they're not.

"I *am* retired," Blair said. "If I keep saying it, it makes it true." Her voice flattened. "What do you want, Drew? I'm busy keeping Lachlan from reorganizing my store."

Drew chuckled. "Say hello to Lach for me. Haven't seen him in years. We have a ghostly matter I wanted to ask you about." He briefly ran through what we'd been dealing with and then asked, "Why would Nora seek us out to help her, then block Ava from animating her bones?"

"Sometimes ghosts want one thing until their rage takes over. Like, they get moments of clarity and seek help to free themselves from wherever they're stuck, even if they're the ones who stuck themselves there. The clarity never lasts long before they're completely taken over by their rage and the need for vengeance." Blair paused as if thinking over our situation. "It sounds like you need to get her spirit out of the castle before she can move on. If she won't come out willingly or by magical force, you'll have to find something she wants bad enough to leave the castle for."

It made sense. We thanked Blair and hung up. All we had to do now was find out what Nora wanted that we could use to lure her out of the castle.

It was late when we got back, dirty and tired, it was to a full-blown haunted house. Dread clotted my throat as the hairs on my arms stood up. Nora had put two and two together. She must've known we'd released her laird and his mistress, and she was beyond mad about it.

The moment we stepped into the lobby, all of the stuff on the walls came alive and tried to attack us. The poor front desk clerk, Niko, cowered under his desk. At least it was late enough that other guests were asleep in their rooms, hopefully *not* being haunted by their wall art. I didn't want any humans hurt by this raging psycho of a ghost.

Boy, was she livid. Nora appeared in the doorway to the dining area. We rushed over to see her go toward the tables, which were already set for the next morning's breakfast. "You ruined everything and I'm going to make you pay!"

The irate ghost swept plates from a table, and they flew in a spinning arc toward Olivia. She screamed and threw up her hands, blasting the plates with her magic. The shards of glass swept on either side of her and fell to the ground. I had to find a way to stop this. Or at least get us out of here.

Suddenly, I remembered the door to the secret passage we'd found the day before. I grabbed Olivia's hand and pulled us toward the bookcase next to the large fireplace, running through the lobby. "Drew, come on!"

Wind whipped around us, and debris flew past us in a blur. Someone screamed as metal objects soared overhead and crashed through windows. We plunged into the hidden stairwell, darkness enveloping us.

With the help of an orb, we ran up three flights of stairs. At the top, I listened as everything fell silent.

When we finally reached our room, via the secret passage, Snoozer and Lucy were lying on the bed. Snoozer looked remotely interested to see us. Lucy was bathing herself, despite the fact that we'd used magic to make sure they were clean.

Figured they'd make it to the room before we did. Ignoring the cats, Drew, Olivia, and I barricaded the door and the windows with salt. Then we plopped onto the bed, against a protesting Lucy's wishes, and tried to catch our breath.

We were in for a long night.

CHAPTER FOURTEEN

The next morning over breakfast, which we ate in our room, Olivia, Drew, and I made a plan to get Nora's ghost out of the castle.

We'd gone through the portal and slept in our own beds, coming back occasionally to check on the castle and make sure she hadn't killed anyone. With us gone, she seemed to have calmed down.

Once we had her outside, I could force her spirit into her bones. It was getting her out that was tricky.

After breakfast, we tiptoed through the castle, wary and nervous that Nora would pop out and attempt to behead us again with one of the swords hanging on the wall.

The presence of all the other people must've been calming her, or at least making her wary because we managed to get out the front door without anyone losing as much as a fingernail.

We hopped in a taxi and headed to Malcolm Jr.'s house. The woman from the cafe the day before had written down his address, so I just gave it to the driver. I was hoping that Malcolm Jr. might have some idea about how to draw his mother's ghost out of the castle. He'd been in his twenties when they'd died. He'd known her a while, longer than almost anyone else alive.

Malcolm Jr. met us at the door. He was a small, wiry man, and he looked exhausted, yet somehow not surprised to see three American strangers on his stoop. "What can I do for you?"

"Hello, Laird Malcolm. My name is Ava. This is my husband Drew, and my good friend Olivia." I gave him a sad smile. "We're here about your parents."

With a sigh, he unlatched the screen door. "You mean their ghosts?"

I nodded and Olivia said a little too cheerily, "Yep."

Malcolm's shoulders slumped. "You'd better come in." He led us into his living room without saying much.

Drew, Olivia, and I sat on the sofa while

Malcolm eased into the armchair. "I've always known my parents were haunting the place. I could feel them there, like a weight on my chest. Even all the way out here, so far from the village." His home was on the other side of the village from the castle, and a good way up in the hills past that.

He continued, "But I never knew what to do. It was my life's curse, knowing what happened to them, what they did. Besides, who would ever believe me that ghosts were real?"

"Your mother came to me a few nights ago asking me to help them. That's what I plan to do," I said. "The problem is that she refuses to leave the castle. We believe that when her rage takes over, she loses all sense of helping herself. We think, and hope, that if we can get her ghost out of the castle, her power will be reduced. Is there anything that she would want badly enough to leave the castle?"

"Her husband." He frowned and added, "Looking back, I realize she had an unhealthy obsession with my father."

I slouched in my seat and thought about pouting for a nano-second. "We *were* able to help your father and Holly to move on. So his ghost is gone. He's at peace."

I waited a moment while tears filled Malcolm

Jr.'s eyes. "That's nice to hear," he whispered. "Excuse me."

He left the room for a few minutes, coming back with red eyes.

"Is there anything else you can think of?" I asked.

He cleared his throat and dabbed his nose with a hankie in his hand. "My grandson, Osker, looks just like my father. Perhaps he could help you lure her out," Malcolm said. "He knows the story. My son thinks I'm an old fool, but Oskar always believed me."

"That could actually work," Olivia said, eyeing me. I plucked the thought right out of her head. Not literally because I wasn't telepathic, but I knew that look. It was the *we'll improvise with magic* look.

"Could you get him to meet us at the castle? We'll explain everything to him when he gets there." I stood and held out my hand. "Tell him not to come inside. We'll come out to him."

Malcolm nodded. "I think he'd do that. And he's off work today. I'll call him right away."

I sighed in relief. "Thank you for your help."

He stood and smiled, taking my hand in both of his. "Thank you for helping them move on."

"Just pray we can pull it off." Even if that didn't work, I wasn't going to give up easily. I couldn't leave knowing Nora was still pushing women down the stairs. If we couldn't get her to move on, I didn't want to think about what she'd do without her husband and Holly there to torment. One way or another, we were getting Nora out of that castle, even if it meant calling in the un-retired hunters. Or the devil himself. He'd probably have a trick or two up his sleeve. Hopefully, this would work, and we could all move on with our lives.

Drew, Olivia, and I were quiet on the ride back to the castle. We were each contemplating how magic could help get Nora's ghost out of the building. You know, just in case Oskar pretending to be his great-grandfather didn't work.

Everyone needs a backup plan.

When we arrived back at the castle, it was eerily quiet. No one was around, which would make getting Nora's ghost out easier, but also more dangerous because there would be no witnesses if something went wrong. Where was everyone?

"Let's get out of here," Olivia whispered. "I don't have a good feeling." We waited outside for a while, then decided to walk around the castle once to pass the time. When we came around the last corner, arriving in the front again, Oskar was waiting for us.

Wow. He did look just like Malcolm senior. So

much so that they could've been twins. For the first time, I started to have a little hope that this plan would work. Maybe we wouldn't have to call Luci after all.

As long as we could convince Nora her husband had come back for her. That'd be the hard part.

After I explained everything to Oskar, he agreed to help us. "My grandfather filled me in on the way." He still looked a little skeptical of the whole thing, but I was glad he was playing along. Even if it was probably only to humor Malcolm Jr.

We led Oskar to a secluded garden in the back, which we'd picked out on our walk just a few moments before.

Olivia portaled to the cemetery and returned with Nora's bones, which, thanks to the practice she'd gotten last night, only took her mere minutes.

She set them on the ground a few feet from us. Then I turned to Oskar to go over the plan again. "You're pretending to be your great grandfather, Laird Malcolm. Just call Nora, using her name." Umm, had he had a pet name for her? I hoped not. We should've looked at earlier entries of her diary to see if it mentioned it. Too late now. "We'll take care of the rest."

Olivia added, "Tell her you've come back for her."

Oskar nodded. "I think I know what to say."

I stretched out my hands and tried to create a protective circle. One that would trap her once she crossed the barrier. The circle formed around us and quickly disappeared. Crap. Stupid faulty magic.

My mom said that my power glitches would go away once the baby was born, and the lineage magic evened out between me and the new girl in the family.

I tried again and it held a little longer. Then Drew moved closer to me and took my hand. "Try again."

I did and the circle slammed closed and stayed. "Thanks," I said and kissed him on the cheek. Then I motioned to Oskar, who was staring at us like we were nuts. He couldn't see the barrier, so it probably looked to him like I was constipated. "Go ahead and call out to her."

He gave a single nod before facing the north side of the castle. "Nora, it's Malcolm. I'm here." He spoke loudly but didn't yell. His accent thickened as well, and his voice did remarkably resemble Malcolm Seniors, or at least how I remembered it had sounded last night.

A long couple of seconds passed in silence. I was about to tell Oskar to try again when I heard a scream that would put a banshee to shame. I jerked my gaze up and watched Nora's ghost careen out of the side of the building. She wasted no time. Her rage was so hot she didn't sense the circle at all. She shot right into the middle of it, to my delight.

Oh, my. She was not happy to see us at all. She studied Oskar's face, squinting and cocking her head. "Malcolm?"

The bright sunlight made it even more apparent she was transparent, but it was clear enough to see that her face was etched in anger as she rounded on me. I reacted instantly, praying to the universe that my powers wouldn't fail me now.

I took a deep breath, pulled the energy from my core, and reached for the necromancer magic that hummed in my blood. It spilled from my hands and flew through the air, tendrils reaching for Nora's ghost. With one gigantic yank, I forced Nora's spirit into the pile of bones on the ground.

Like Holly and Malcolm, Nora's skeleton rose and became animated. It wasn't funny this time.

I'd used so much power to compensate for my faulty magic that I'd really whammied her. Her bones fleshed out so that she looked like before she died. She'd really been beautiful.

She looked down at herself and calmed, then turned to Oskar. Reaching out she asked, "Malcolm?"

Oskar shook his head. "I'm sorry. I'm Oskar, your great-grandson."

Her face softened. "Malcolm Junior's boy?"

He nodded. "Close enough. They say Father looks like you, but Grandfather and I look like Malcolm Senior."

Nora pulled Oskar into her arms for a long embrace, and then she turned to us.

"Thank you," she said. "Thank you for giving me the chance to say goodbye."

And with that, she was gone. Finally free. Her spirit floated, less energetically than Malcolm and Holly had. More peacefully. At the same time, her body turned back into bones in Oskar's arms.

"Ugh," he said and dropped the bones. "I mean..."

"No." I laughed. "Ugh is an appropriate response."

CHAPTER FIFTEEN

It was Halloween night, and Olivia and I were preening in front of the bathroom mirror. Olivia's dark purple velvet gown set off her blond hair. My black one seemed to make my usually too-pale complexion glow in this wonderful castle lighting. Everything was magical here, especially now that the malevolent ghost was gone.

Sam, Wade, Winnie, Alfred, and my parents walked through the portal mirror. They were all dressed up. Sam and Wade went with the 1800s vampire theme. No one but us knew the fangs were real. "I love it!" I chirped.

Mom and Dad were dressed as Gomez and Morticia Addams. "You both look amazing." Mom had glamoured her hair black, so it looked so natural like it was how she always looked.

Winnie and Alfred—I still couldn't wrap my head around them being a couple— were dressed like cave people. Of course, Winnie had gone with her normal state of undress. Her furs barely covered anything. And Alfred, who on his own would've dressed far more conservatively, wore only a loin-cloth, which he kept tugging at. "You two look sexy as hell." That was the perfect thing to say to Aunt Winnie, who was obsessed with her new body.

Not that I blamed her.

Luci and Phira had Sammie in Faery for a Samhain celebration. Wally, Michelle, Zoey, Larry, Devan, and Jessica were hanging at the house handing out candy and watching scary movies.

"Oh my gosh, you guys look great." I stepped out of the bathroom and had to squeeze by everyone. The room had gotten smaller with my family there. "Are we ready to head down to the ballroom?" Everyone was in agreement, and so looking forward to a haunting good time now that the ghosts were friendly and not stabby.

The ballroom was filled with tables covered with thick red cloth. Printed on the fabric were the outlines of rib cages with the words Rest in Peace quilted into them. Large skeleton garlands made of paper streamers dropped from the ceiling and waved gently above us.

I looked around and smiled at the others. "They did a nice job, didn't they?" I said. Everyone nodded and smiled back, seeming to agree despite the hard time we'd been through.

We found a table close to the dance floor and ordered drinks. Whether Drew knew it or not, he was dancing with me, frequently.

And as soon as the first slow song came on, I dragged him out onto the dance floor.

Our hips swayed in unison as we held each other. Our eyes closed, our breath felt hot and heavy, and our hearts raced. I felt his as much as my own. Such a wonderful feeling, to be so connected to Drew.

"I love you, husband," I whispered.

He held me tighter and nipped at my ear. "Love you more, wife."

"Oh, not possible."

"It's possible."

"Time will tell," I teased. "We work well together. I'm glad we were able to get Nora to move on."

"If we hadn't, we'd have to come back in ten years

and try again." He flashed me a smile before pulling me even closer.

I was about to ask him if he missed hunting when my phone buzzed in my dress pocket. Without breaking our dance, I pulled it out and answered. "Hello?"

"Um, Mom, Drew's grandmother was just here looking for you," Wallie said.

Then Drew made a noise before saying, "What is *she* doing here?"

I looked up in time to see Pearl entering the ballroom. "She's here," I told Wallie. "Thanks for the warning."

I hung up and Drew and I made our way off of the dance floor and to our table. It didn't bode well that the matriarch of the hunters had made her way to the Halloween ball. She certainly hadn't been invited.

Pearl didn't bother with a polite greeting. I hadn't really expected her to. It wasn't her style. "You know that tentacle monster we fought at your rehearsal dinner?"

Oh, no. Please don't tell me he has a brother.

Drew worked his jaw and then said, "Yeah."

"Well, his twin sister was spotted off the coast of Owl's Head." Pearl glanced from Drew to me, then back to Drew. Crap. That was *really* close to Shipton.

My husband picked up his drink, took a sip, and set it down. "And?"

Pearl glared at her grandson. "You and Ava will be going to take care of it."

I had my drink halfway to my mouth. "We're doing what now?"

Pearl turned her glare to me. "You are a hunter now, Ava Walker. You married a hunter. You bonded with a hunter."

I gaped at her. We'd never told his family that we'd bonded.

"Oh, yes." She put her hands on her hips. "If you don't think I didn't see that first thing when I arrived at your house, you've got another think coming."

Super. It looked like I was going after a tentacle monster.

MORE PARANORMAL WOMEN'S FICTION BY L.A. BORUFF

Witching After Forty (Paranormal Women's Fiction)

A Newly-Webs Midlife

Fanged After Forty (Paranormal Women's Fiction)

Bitten in the Midlife
Staked in the Midlife
Masquerading in the Midlife
Bonded in the Midlife
Dominating in the Midlife
Wanted in the Midlife

Packless in Seattle

The Midlife Prelude
The Midlife Shift

Prime Time of Life (Paranormal Women's Fiction)

COMPLETE SERIES
Series Boxed Set
Complete Series Volume 1
Complete Series Volume 2
Borrowed Time
Stolen Time
Just in Time
Hidden Time
Nick of Time

Magical Midlife in Mystic Hollow (Paranormal Women's Fiction)

Karma's Spell

Karma's Shift

Karma's Spirit

Karma's Sense

Karma's Stake

Karma's Source

Shifting Into Midlife (Paranormal Women's Fiction)

Pack Bunco Night

Alpha Males and Other Shift

The Cat's Meow

Midlife Mage (Paranormal Women's Fiction)

Unfazed

Unbowed

Unsaid

An Immortal Midlife

An Immortal Midlife (Paranormal Women's Fiction)

COMPLETE SERIES

Series Boxed Set

Fatal Forty

Fighting Forty
Finishing Forty

Immortal West (Paranormal Women's Fiction)

Undead
Hybrid
Fae

The Meowing Medium

The Meowing Medium (Paranormal Cozy)

COMPLETE SERIES

Series Boxed Set Coming Soon

Secrets of the Specter
Gifts of the Ghost
Pleas of the Poltergeist

An Unseen Midlife (Paranormal Women's Fiction Reverse Harem)

Bloom In Blood
Dance In Night
Bask In Magic
Surrender In Dreams

ABOUT L.A. BORUFF

USA Today Bestselling Author L.A. (Lainie) Boruff lives in East Tennessee with her husband, three children, and an ever-growing number of cats. She loves reading, watching TV, and procrastinating by browsing Facebook. L.A.'s passions include vampires, food, and listening to heavy metal music. She once won a Harry Potter trivia contest based on the books and lost one based on the movies. She has two bands on her bucket list that she still hasn't seen: AC/DC and Alice Cooper. Feel free to send tickets.

ABOUT LIA DAVIS

USA Today bestselling author Lia Davis spends most of her time writing racy romance and witty women's fiction, the majority of which takes place in fantasy worlds full of magic and mayhem. She prides herself on her ability to craft strong and sassy heroines, emotionally intelligent alpha heroes, and rich, expansive universes that readers want to visit again and again.

She is the mastermind behind the bestselling Ashwood Falls Series and the co-author of the beloved Witching After Forty Series.

She currently resides in Florida where she's working on her very own happily-ever-after with her supportive husband and spends her free time doting on a pack of feisty felines and her loving family.

Find all of Lia's online hangouts here:
https://solo.to/authorliadavis
Check out the official Davis Raynes Merch Etsy Store:
https://www.etsy.com/shop/davisraynesmerch